Metaphorosis

November 2019

Beautifully made speculative fiction

Also from Metaphorosis

Score – an SFF symphony

Reading 5X5: Readers' Edition
Reading 5X5: Writers' Edition

Best Vegan Science Fiction & Fantasy

Best Vegan SFF 2018
Best Vegan SFF 2017
Best Vegan SFF 2016

Metaphorosis Magazine

Metaphorosis: Best of 2018
Metaphorosis: Best of 2017
Metaphorosis: Best of 2016

Metaphorosis 2018: The Complete Stories
Metaphorosis 2017: The Complete Stories
Metaphorosis 2016: Nearly Complete Stories

Monthly issues

by B. Morris Allen

Susurrus
Allenthology: Volume I
Tocsin: and other stories
Start with Stones: collected stories
Metaphorosis: a collection of stories

Metaphorosis

November 2019

edited by
B. Morris Allen

ISSN: 2573-136X (online)
ISBN: 978-1-64076-151-3 (e-book)
ISBN: 978-1-64076-152-0 (paperback)

Metaphorosis
a magazine of speculative fiction
from
Metaphorosis Publishing

Neskowin

November 2019

Rooks on Sundays

Jack Neel Waddell

"You never liked to play chess with me," she says.

The board lies on a tray across her bed. Pillows prop her up slightly, just enough to see the pieces.

She reaches out a wrinkled hand, skin both pale and blotched brown, like the flesh of an apple left out too long. She grabs a rook that she carved, perhaps twenty-five years ago, from purpleheart wood. Today she remembers how it moves.

"I know how much you love it, Mom," I say, the word still feeling awkward in my mouth. It took me weeks to even say it.

We play until the end of visiting hours. She frowns as a nurse comes in. She weakly tries to push him away as he hooks her oxygen mask back over her face, clasping the straps behind her head within the milkweed-seed wisps of her hair.

I walk out of her room and toward the door of St. Agatha's hospice.

"You have to sign out, ma'am," calls the registration nurse after me.

The log book is open, with the heading, "Patient: Ella Reilly."

I sign Katherine Reilly, the only name on the list going back every Sunday for pages.

I've hidden the case in a park a few blocks away. A few cherries are blooming, but a chilling drizzle drives away any strolling couples.

I press the button on the front of the case to return.

I tuck the case back under the bench in my garage shop. Then I get inside my Corolla and drive.

There's one other place I go on Sundays.

It isn't raining here, now. The sun shines with vernal tenderness through the willows onto a pair of monument stones, dated only months apart. I place butter-yellow mums on my dearest James's grave, the one on the right. Kay, our daughter, buried in the other, never cared for flowers.

She injured her back when a Land Rover drove her into a ditch on her way to the coffee shop. She was taking an extra shift to pay us rent, which I imposed when she refused to sign up for classes at the community college.

The doctor gave her pills, which ran out. She found more, then she took too many.

James always blamed me for the gulf between us and our daughter. He left me after Kay's funeral, but his heart gave out before the divorce was final, whether from grief or stress or coincidence.

I wish I could take my case back to one or any moment during that time, to pull them back to me. Or, if not that, just to have them again as I push them from me — an arm's length away is closer than six feet deep. But the past is Hermetically sealed, even to my machine.

I've already purchased the bare plot to the right of James, but I won't need it for twenty-eight years. Now I'm saving up for the Catholic rest home in town, the best in the county, since I will have no one to tend to me but myself, and only on Sundays.

I drive back to my shop. Small blocks of exotic wood lie scattered on the workbench. I reach for a piece of purpleheart I rounded on the lathe, then hesitate. Instead, I select ebony. I pick up a gouge and carve.

Slivers of the past fall away with each splinter. Soon I think of nothing but the piece hidden in the grain and, after a while, I finish the crenellated parapet of a rook.

"What's this?" she asks as I hand her the box. It's wide, long, and thin, like a box of chocolates.

"A gift, Mom," I say. "Open it."

She pulls the ribbon and lifts the top. Laid out in four rows is the chess set I've made over the past month, of ebony and olivewood. She picks up the kings of each color.

"They're beautiful, Kay," she says.

She smiles, eyes beaming, and it warms my heart.

"You made these?" she asks.

I nod, with a strangely proud smile spreading across my face. But her eyebrows draw together in suspicion. She turns her eyes up and left, as if she's trying to call something elusive to mind.

"Mom?"

She looks at me, and I see something change in her.

She puts the pieces back in the box and places it aside, then leans out and places a pale hand on my own. She looks into my eyes, and I into hers. I see the peanut-brown of her irises, not the forest-floor hue of Kay's, and I know she sees the same because within her eyes shines a spark of recognition. A spark that fades into sorrow.

"You're so good to visit me," she says, voice breaking. "All we've got is each other."

See Jack Neel Waddell's story "Rooks on Sundays" online at Metaphorosis.
If you liked it, leave a comment. Authors love that!
Remember to subscribe to our e-mail updates so you'll know when new stories are posted.

About the story

The impetus of this story was Heinlein's "'—All You Zombies—'", although they have little obvious in common. While Heinlein's masterpiece is a gutwrenching puzzle, it laid bare one element I wanted to meditate upon — how manipulating people isn't always about the control you have over them, but can be about struggling against the ever-diminishing influence in your environment and even your own mind. That is ever more the case when the person you are manipulating is yourself.

A question for the author

Q: What would your animal totem be?

A: Do you choose your totem, or does it choose you? I suspect the latter, in which case the answer is a raccoon. I have unintentionally shared too many a backwoods meal with these little beasts to say any different. I am defeated; they are smarter than me. I will aspire to their cunning, and when I one day pass beyond the veil, perhaps they will allow me to join them as the least of their number.

About the author

Jack Neel Waddell is a Southern writer, physicist, and educator. He lives with his wife, baby, and furred companions in Arkansas, where he enriches young minds (but only to reactor-grade levels, he swears).

gildthetruth.wordpress.com

Via Dolorosa

Christine Lucas

"Your father crapped himself," croaks her aunt's ghost. "Go clean him up!"

"Yes, Aunt Katina." Father craps himself every other hour; Maro needs to finish the bills first. But the numbers won't add up. Father's pension isn't enough anymore.

"Such a worthless daughter," mutters the ghost. "I envy your mother, who's not around to watch!"

Of all the ghosts in this damned house, Aunt Katina had to be the talkative one. Maro shoves the bills into a drawer. The chair creaks as she stands, the floor creaks as she walks, and the ever-flowing mist of ethereal forms parts as she crosses the low-roofed, dimly-lit rooms to Father's room.

If he's soiled himself, he didn't notice. Nor has his mother's ghost, Maro's grandmother, who sits beside him knitting with ghostly yarn and needles. Every night, all night. Only once did Maro spot Yaya standing over Father's head. Her ethereal lips moved, forming voiceless words, as she did before the cancer that robbed her of breath robbed her of life too. Was she singing? Praying? Spinning one of her many tales, her own bedtime stories with threads from many eras—the Twelve, the Trinity, before? Many gods have trodden these lands, many faiths merged and mingled, and Yaya knew tales of them all.

Maro misses her tales and her voice. Now Yaya's form flickers when Maro turns on the bedside lamp, as if startled by the sudden illumination, and fades back into the shadows. Father only mumbles, drowsy after his evening pills. Where has his brilliant mind gone, his deep voice, his laughter? Into his overflowing diaper and his soiled hands?

"Ah, Father..."

Maro longs for past times, easier times, when flunked homework was her worst fear. Now, decades later, the dust on every surface in the room mocks her yearning. That same dust seems to sparkle and rise into the air and swirl into the ghostly forms, and she likes to track their languid journeys through her parents' house. A respite for her tired mind from the daily tasks that involve latex gloves and diapers.

There, a ghostly cat darts after a long-gutted mouse who sprints into a hole. Yaya is back, spinning another tale with the clickety-clack of ghostly needles, a tongue Maro hasn't yet deciphered. All around, forms with no faces stroll through Father's bedchamber. Ethereal flies mingle with real ones, their buzz no less annoying.

Father's eyes flutter when she pulls fresh sheets up to his chin, to keep the April chill away. A heartbeat later, he snores. Maro piles up the trash and the soiled linen.

"Goodnight, Father. Goodnight, Yaya," she tells the ghost, and almost drops her load.

A new ghost shimmers beside Yaya. It's a young woman, dressed in a sleeveless floral dress, plump, with a pleasant round face and short, curly hair. Maro had a similar dress when she was around this ghost's age—most girls did, back in the eighties. But she doesn't remember this late-hour visitor. Could she be one of Father's former patients? Her ghost wouldn't be the first to come and pay their respects to their now-bedridden physician.

Maro's sigh ripples through the mist of dust and ghosts. Does it matter, who this one is? She'll be gone shortly—like most of them are. Even Mother's ghost doesn't linger—thank the Virgin it doesn't. Once, Maro caught a glimpse of her mother's face with her lips sewn shut, like something out of a horror film—like punishment for a sin too terrible to speak of.

No.

Maro shuts her eyes, balls her fists. It wasn't her. Mother is with God now. Not... *elsewhere*. When Maro looks up, the new ghost has vanished.

Yaya has stopped her knitting, her empty eyes now staring into thin air.

"Go get a job, you lazy sow," Aunt Katina croaks overhead.

"Good morning to you," mumbles Maro over the stove, warming up Father's tea.

From across the house her father cries that he's hungry, and hits the wall with his cane. It's the way the world works in these parts: dutiful daughters look after aging parents, cook for and feed them. And, if, by chance, one extra sedative falls into Father's handful of pills, no harm done. Better this way, calm and snoring, his hands away from his catheter and his cane away from her back.

Now she needs to find work.

Maro zips her jacket up to the chin. What job can she possibly find in this god-forsaken town? Things were different when she was growing up. When the trade route from Athens and Piraeus to Bulgaria passed through, before the interstate, when the young folk hadn't left, before austerity. Not anymore. There are no tourist sites to exploit around here; only the desolate ruins of the *Nekyomanteion*, the Oracle where ancient priests consulted the dead. Just a field of broken white marble now. And the dead still linger, but create no jobs. Especially none for middle-aged florists. Madonna knows she liked her job—a respectable lady's employment, Aunt Katina used to say. But she couldn't even keep that job, could she? As if it were her fault the bank foreclosed on the shop and she had to move back home, when the economy took a plunge ten years ago.

Maro stops ten steps out of the garden door. *Deep breaths. Wipe your eyes.* The neighbors think her weird already, their gossip following her since childhood. She doesn't want to hear them today, the ignorant, blissful fools. How she's unkempt, and a spinster, and *wind-blown*, and *light-of-shadow*, and bird-brained for consorting with the Unseen— with everything that stretches beyond their simple minds and simple lives: the winks of the nymphs and dryads, the shuffling of undead feet at the crossroads, the many ghosts of her house and every house she visits, and the spirits of soldiers of too many wars—those who died, and those who didn't and still wished for death, mourning their lost innocence.

Will she too one day join them, seeking some peace for her troubled soul?

Anger swells within her with each determined step downhill, so Maro keeps her eyes on the ground. Enough of the Unseen already. She turns right past the Church of St. Sophia, where once, before the Romans, the Byzantines, and the Ottomans, Athena's temple stood. The town's post office isn't far; the clerk there, Martha, Aunt Katina's old schoolmate, is Queen Gossip-monger in these parts. If there's work to be found—under-the-table, discreet work—she'll know. Especially now, with many expats flocking back into town for Easter.

One deep inhale to let the crisp April breeze cool her flushed face, and Maro pushes the post office's door open. It's empty, this early, but for the clerk and one of her friends. They sit at a side table sipping coffee from the shop across the street. They hold their ever-rolling tongues the moment she steps in, and exchange a glance.

Gut-knotting envy robs Maro of breath. She envies all that they are and all that they have: their lacquered nails, the overpriced coffee, their perfectly plucked eyebrows, the hours they can waste. She enters their domain a beggar, famished and practically barefoot in cheap sneakers. And like a proper beggar, Maro swallows her pride and begs. The remnants of her dignity peel off her with every cutting remark of Martha's honeyed tongue, but she stands her ground.

Ten minutes later, after endless not-really-pleasantries about Father's health and how things are tough all-around, Maro leaves with an address. One of her old schoolmates—Zoe something, a retired school teacher now—needs domestic help to put her recently deceased uncle's house in order. Maro doesn't recognize the name —perhaps she was a year or two older than Maro? But her school years are lifetimes away, and her memories of that time as elusive as the ghosts in her home.

She passes gardens in early bloom, lilacs and daisies and the first buds of roses. The prettiest roses bloomed around St. George's Feast on April 23rd, Mother used to say. Father's nameday, and their home flooded with spring's first roses every year. Not anymore. Not since Mother died, and even before that. When did Spring diminish in their home? She thinks... she thinks that the chill entered shortly before she left for Athens to learn her trade. And with every passing season, the chill claimed more of Mother and Aunt Katina, and now gnaws on Father.

Blessed be the Virgin for having spared Yaya. That remarkable woman, whose every last wrinkle shone with kindness, passed away when Maro was barely a teenager. The first ghost she ever saw—Yaya appeared to her shortly after her passing, one crisp April evening with the lilacs in full bloom. And now, their scent and the sound of Yaya's needles are like a balm to her troubled soul.

Zoe's uncle's home is a two-story building with a small garden filled with lilac bushes. Perhaps it is a divine sign that she'll be welcomed here, and she'll find what she needs. Her feet are lighter when she climbs the few steps two at a time, and her knock on the door is steady and brisk.

The woman who answers the door wears the face of the ghost who visited Father last night.

No, Zoe doesn't have—nor did she have—an older sister. No, she never had a cousin or daughter who died young. From a careful glance at family pictures on the walls, Zoe's late mother looks nothing like last night's visitor. And Zoe has never been in any war. Maro bites her tongue so as not to ask Zoe's uncle; conversing with ghosts won't make for a good first impression.

Now Zoe, plump and grey-haired, limps around her own dust and ghosts. Her steps are slow, cautious, as if not to disturb the gliding forms around her. She holds herself with a slight hunch, remnant of a youth when puberty bred shame. Maro remembers that time all too well herself. Breasts should be covered either by loose clothes or hunched backs, so to not attract attention. No man cares for middle-aged, saggy breasts now, but shame cemented their backbones in this *respectable* curve.

"...just some light dusting, and boxing everything that needs to be donated and stored and..."

Maro wants to pay attention to Zoe's mellow voice, but her eyes keep darting back to her uncle's ghost, who's lounging in his worn armchair, scratching a crotch that shouldn't itch. It's been years since she last saw him; he was friends with Father once, in another life, when friends and family gathered at their garden on Easter Sunday for skewered lamb and wine and dance and song. Back then, his face shone with the deep, robust color of one bottle of wine too many. His ample belly overflowed from pants worn too low, and he was the first to lend his sonorous voice to every song.

And now, his ghost shines with a sickly yellow tint: his eyes, his skin, his fingertips, and he wears stained clothes three sizes too big. The gold ring with the big red stone hangs loose from his little finger, his nail crooked and claw-like, but picks his ethereal nose with the devotion of his living self. Hatred glints in eyes deeply set on his emaciated face; hatred and disgust at his niece. He keeps mouthing one word, but no sound comes out.

Virgin help them, is he calling *her* a whore?

"... and some help with the groceries. Would twenty per day be sufficient?" Zoe's voice quivers when she articulates the number, as if talking money is rude.

"Yes!" Maro doesn't care whether it's rude, whether this house too crawls with ghosts. Hell, she wouldn't care if Zoe's dead uncle spent eternity calling her a whore. Dignity is overvalued. With Easter Sunday two weeks away, perhaps she'll manage something resembling a feast.

"Good." Zoe smiles back, a timid smile on a face that seems more accustomed to grief than mirth. "I don't suppose you can start today?"

"Ah." Maro checks her watch; almost two hours since she slipped Father that pill. He should be waking soon. If he doesn't see her when he wakes, there's no calming him down afterwards. She rubs her arms; the recent bruises from his cane still ache. And God forbid he try to get up and break his brittle bones. "I need to go check on Father. But that won't be an issue tomorrow."

For a second, Zoe's face darkens. Gliding shadows curtain her face. For a heartbeat, Zoe's dead face stares back at Maro: opaque eyes, ashen skin, her head bandaged in greying shroud. Zoe's uncle cackles.

Maro thanks Zoe and flees. Virgin help her, she'll come back. She must.

And so she does return, with Father tucked in safely and tightly in his bed. Aunt Katina doesn't like it one bit.

"What kind of a daughter are you? How dare you put your father in restraints?"

Perched upon the framed tapestry over Father's bed, she wags a ghostly finger. "I'm so glad your poor mother isn't—"

"Oh, shut up!" *Mother?* A ghost too faint even by ghostly standards glides over the bed. Only the thick threads of lips sewn together are clear.

"Ah, truth hurts, doesn't it?" Aunt Katina crows.

Hah! Truth! More like rudeness. But dear auntie has a point—ghosts, when they choose to speak, cannot lie. Yaya told her so before she died—some rule of God's creation none of them are privy to. What other rules she has yet to discover?

Maro tests the restraints. Not too tight, to dig into his flesh, but—hopefully—not too loose either.

"I'll tell him," coos the ghost. "Once he wakes up and you're not here, I'll tell him what you did." Her voice quivers with the promise of pain.

"So tell him." Maro grabs her purse and heads to the door. Fathers aims his cane at her for imaginary slights every day anyway. "If you want me to stay with Father, why don't you go work? You know, *work?* The one thing you never did in your life?"

"That's why I got a husband," screeches the ghost as Maro opens the door. "You know, the one thing *you* never had in *your* life?"

Maro slams the door and heads downhill, her eyes on the ground, her palms balled to fists by her hips. Aunt Katina's last retort burns her deeper than it should. Snorting like a distressed bull, she heads to the small grocery store to pick up the things in Zoe's list.

Inside the store, she almost drops her basket when she bumps into Gossip Queen Martha at the turn of an aisle. Today, she has her oldest daughter in tow, Maro's former classmate, Nina. Nina has her eyes and thumbs glued on her phone, her hair dyed Viking blonde.

Martha measures Maro from greying hair to worn sneakers. "So, you took the job? How magnanimous of you. I assume your father is better now? Will we see him in church? I miss his voice singing Kassiani's hymn. The best cantor we've ever had."

"We'll see." Maro evades an answer. Father did enjoy volunteering as a cantor in Papa-Nikolas' church. And now his beautiful voice has waned to moans and raspy cries, and she's stored his dark suit away, to be worn one final time. Yearning almost chokes her. "He did love that hymn."

The woman befallen in many sins... The hymn's first line rings clear in her ears. Not in Father's voice but Zoe's, soft and riddled with unspeakable shame. It robs Maro of breath.

"Perhaps he'd love to sing it for your friend Zoe." Martha spits the name as though it were manure on her tongue.

"Mother!" Now does Nina look up. "Enough!" She drags Martha away.

And Maro stands speechless, clutching a roll of paper towels on her chest.

Maro pieces together part of Zoe's secret over the following days through muffled gossip behind her back at the grocer's, at the baker's, at the butcher's. At home, her dear auntie is unusually tight-lipped.

And now, as Maro stores away tome after tome of Zoe's uncle's library, she watches Zoe out of the corner of her eye. *Home-wrecker*, they call her. Did that gentle woman once have an affair with a married man here in town? If Zoe knows of Maro's sleuthing, she doesn't show it.

Zoe wears her dignity like the ghosts around them wear their shrouds. Day after day, she offers nothing but quiet kindness over the books with the words of Homer and Pindar and Euripides and Sophocles.

Sometimes they joke, and sometimes they chat, and sometimes they sit sipping coffee in dusty but comfortable silence. During those few, precious moments, Maro dares to wear her own face. Neither the books nor Zoe judge her for the audacity to shed her predestined face of daughter, caregiver, spinster. The prospect of a life *afterwards* pokes out its head and it does so riddled with guilt. After Father's death.

Father. The echo of the town's gossip grapples with her again. Could Father be that married man? But Aunt Katina wouldn't keep silent about *that*. Perhaps she got pregnant and Father refused to give her an abortion? Such procedures were not only shameful back then, but illegal too. *I'm a scientist, not a butcher,* Father used to say. *Women stupid enough to get knocked up can go to the quacks in Athens.*

And Zoe had left for Athens and never came back. Until now.

Maro's head hurts. She spends too much energy, too much time, on something that shouldn't be her concern. And hour by hour, in the house Zoe shares with her dead uncle, the books are packed, the old clothes donated to St. Sophia's church, the house dusted and cleaned and prepared for a buyer.

Maro will miss their little effortless talks. Chit-chat over books, over flowers, over recipes, with the fleeting illusion of belonging. Even amidst this swarm of ethereal figures, even with Zoe's uncle's ever-leering stare, Maro has found a place she loves to return to.

On their last day, Zoe surprises her with a table full of food. There's hot coffee, and warm bread, and *halva*, and olives, and those little spicy-sweet breads, *Lazarakia. Oh-my-God, is it Lazarus Saturday already?* The Holy Week starts on Monday, and Maro hasn't picked candles, and has nothing to wear for Easter Mass.

But Father won't be going to church this year. Now Maro plops into the nearest chair, and tries hard—very hard—not to weep. But she does. And does so until she runs out of tears, until she runs out of breath, until a hand holds a tissue under

her nose and another strokes her
shoulder.

Zoe pours her a hot cup of coffee. "Your
father?"

Maro nods and blows her nose.

"Is it bad?" She hands her the cup and
one of the *Lazarakia*.

Her dead uncle scoffs. He's still
lounging on his armchair, a man no more.
Just bones now and cracked skin. He lifts
a cigarette between thumb and index
finger, and inhales with lungs he no
longer has.

Maro gulps down the strong brew, and
still it's less bitter than the brine lining
her throat. She chews on the soft
sweetbread. This time, she manages a
whisper.

"Yes. It's bad."

"I'm sorry," Zoe says, her voice low. A
steady, honest whisper—the first
consolation Maro has received from either
the living or the dead.

"The fuck you are, you shriveled
whore," comes her uncle's retort, who
tosses his cigarette at his niece. It
dissolves before it reaches her. Jerk in
life, jerk in death.

"Thank you." Maro takes another sip.

What did Yaya used to say about Lazarus Saturday? That Jesus' command still echoes on this day, awakened from the clergy's hymns? Not everywhere, though. Acheron used to flow through these parts before the coming of younger deities forced it underground. Here, the thin veil between the worlds lifts on that day. And the dead leave their graves to mingle with the living. Soldiers from the World Wars, old women from the Ottoman occupation, lasses from the Byzantine times walk the streets, seeking to board Charon's boat. But they have no coin to offer the Ferryman. Perhaps Charon too has retired to wherever discharged deities go.

So the dead loiter around, pestering the living, until the first rooster calls the sun up on Palm Sunday.

More ghosts. Just great.

Come evening, Maro sits by Father's side. He looks better tonight, his eyes more focused and he squeezes her hand back. He even managed a smile; a real smile, like those he flashed at her many years ago.

Tonight, Yaya sits across the room, knitting a black vest, as she did every Holy Week, to be worn on Good Friday. This time she does so with ethereal yarn and needles, but the clickity-clack is all too familiar, all too real to Maro's heart. Even Aunt Katina sits quiet at the other side of the bed, her eyes occasionally darting about.

The TV shows through occasional static the evening mass from a nearby cathedral. It comforts Father, who tries to chant along. When he hits the notes right, he squeezes Maro's hand tighter. And she knows that, in this here and now, and probably for the last time, Father is happy.

She lays her head on Father's shoulder, comfortable for once in a long time. She has money for a decent Easter supper, she might even afford new shoes for church. And she has a friend out there, someone who knows she thinks and hurts and yearns like normal people do. Then the lights flicker, and her eyelids flutter along. On TV, the preceding priest calls his flock to attendance for the reading of the Gospel: Lazarus' resurrection.

"Lazarus, come forth," recites the priest, pompous and bored in equal parts.

Another flicker of the lights. Maro sits up. The stale air around her now sizzles with the anticipation of approaching storm. Lightning lingers at every corner of the room. Static crackles at the edges of framed pictures, through the worn threads of the rug, through every cobweb. The shadows brew thunder, but this thunder has a voice and a name: *Charon*.

The lights flicker again and go out. In this sudden, absolute darkness that lingers between this world and all others, a figure appears at the foot of Father's bed. A fleshless arm splinters away from the form that's shadow and darkness and something else—something Eternal. It stretches out, palm up, requesting the fare.

The TV's dark, the priests are silenced, the crucifix above the bed lost in the dark. Maro's heart struggles against the confines of her ribs. She wants out, she wants away. Instead, her fingers rummage through her pockets. She only has a couple of fiver notes and one-euro coins. Charon won't take that, she knows it in her gut he won't, he wants old copper drachmas. She's kept a couple; just in case, she told herself, but now where's the old chest? There's nothing but darkness and the luminous palm awaiting. Will he leave Father behind, if there's no pay? After a few frantic seconds, she digs up a copper penny and reaches out.

Please, she pleads with every galloping heartbeat, for this darkness has robbed her of voice. *Please*.

The hood tilts sideways, counts the fare and finds it wanting with a shake of his head. Maro's cry becomes a gasp as the lights flicker back on. The penny clanks on the floor and rolls away. There's no ghostly ferryman in the room. The TV's back on, but shows only static. She dares a glance on the wall behind her, and the crucifix is still there. Thank heavens, Father remained quiet through all this—whatever *this* was. Perhaps she just dozed off and her tired mind played her a nasty prank. She squeezes Father's hand and he squeezes back. A long sigh leaves her lips but then her breath gets hitched again.

Now the room crawls with ghosts.

They glide all around her, between corners, through the fireplace and the chairs. Long, translucent forms with no faces, they circle the bed. Yaya's ghost has stopped her knitting and watches them with narrowed eyes of starless night. Aunt Katina is frighteningly quiet, her face more drawn than usual. Then, like the chorus of an ancient tragedy, the luminous forms stop their swirl, and their *coryphaeus* steps forward, taking Charon's place at the foot of Father's bed.

A teenage girl's ghost, clad in a floral dress, and it wears Zoe's face.

"I died that day." It is Zoe's voice, but neither soft nor shy. It's steady now—articulate. A ghostly hand holds the torn strap of her dress upwards, as if to cover the bruises on her chest. She raises her other hand but, unlike Charon's, this one points at Father. "You did this to me."

"Whore." Aunt Katina's whisper holds more hatred than any screech should.

If Zoe heard her, she doesn't show it. Her eyes, feverish pits in a face of swirling dust, remains fixed on Father. "I was a child."

"Please." Father's voice trembles, but not from age or disease. It's anger that makes the veins on his bald, spotted head pump. "You got exactly what you wanted."

Zoe's hands stretch out the fabric of her dress, exposing all the stains: grass, dirt, blood. "This? You think I wanted *this*?" Her right hand balls to a fist.

"Kindness was all I wanted. Comfort, from someone I thought family!"

"Nonsense." Father scoffs. When he speaks again, his voice carries the arrogance of his younger self along with the anger of the bedridden husk he's become. "You wanted what all the other whores wanted. To become a doctor's mistress and milk me for all my worth. But I didn't play along, and you cried 'rape'."

Who is this man that wears Father's face? Who is this brute, who speaks with Father's voice? Maro tries to pull her hand away, but Father grips it harder, now hard enough to hurt. She tries to wriggle it free and fails.

"Father, please!"

"Shut up, you ungrateful sow! Katina told me you've befriended this whore! This wicked woman, who tried to break up your parents!"

Maro puts all her strength in her shoulder and arm. She pulls her hand free and wipes his spittle from her face. There's a painful gap in her chest. Little pieces of the puzzle slowly fall in place, and every piece that clicks slices away another part of her. The townsfolk's gossip about Zoe being a home-wrecker. The sudden loss of affection between her parents during that summer long ago. Mother's drawn ways. Her silence. And her ghost.

Here she comes, gliding forth amidst the ethereal chorus, as silent in death as in life. But now her lips are sewn shut.

She knew.

But Yaya didn't. Across the room, she now stands with the other ghosts. Her wrinkled face is unreadable. Her gnarled hands clutch on her chest the thread and needles in a white-knuckled grip. And she measures her son with the eyes of a Fury.

"I died on that day," Zoe says again. "My trust. My childhood. You left me broken and you left me empty. Fragmented in moments: my then, my now, my never. And now your time draws near."

"For what?"

"Admission. Apology. Atonement." Zoe's voice is softer now, but still steady. Every single ghost leans forward, as if waiting for the reply with bated breaths.

"Hah!" Father grips his cane.

Maro sinks deeper in her chair.

But the cane isn't aimed at her, for once; he hefts it as a woodsman's axe and tries to strike down the ghost. His reach is

too short. And what good would it do?
Ghosts don't hurt. They don't bruise. They
don't cry. But Maro does, and she swings
to her right just in time to avoid the
spiteful blow now aimed at her. She falls
on the floor and scurries away, in the
shadow between the mantelpiece and the
wall.

She wants to cover her ears to Father's
yells. She wants to cover her eyes and
forget Mother's lips. She cannot. She
should not. Not with Yaya there, her
skinny body wrapped in the same black
dress she wore all her life. So Maro
focuses on her, tuning everything else out.
When Father throws his cane at Maro, she
reconsiders.

"Stupid cunts, all of you! Leave me be!
No peace, all my life, just your endless
nagging. Now you nag me on my
deathbed?" He raises his fist at Zoe. "And
you, whore. You got what you asked.
What you deserved. That's my admission
and my apology." He falls back down on
his pillow, licking the spittle from his lips.
"Now go away. All of you."

There's a moment of silence heavy with
thunder. Zoe just stares at him, still like a
Caryatis statue, counting his deeds and
his days. No ghost dares move, no speck

of dust dares to swirl floor-bound. Maro holds her breath, trying to endure the crushing stillness around her.

Yaya moves forward, her petite frame straight, her needles in her right hand. She glides forward through wooden frame and mattress, through yellow skin and brittle bone and dying flesh. Now the Crone, now the Matriarch, now the Fury.

Father looks up, his eyes wide. "*Mana?* What are you doing?"

Yaya hefts the needles as a dagger and plunges them in Father's chest.

Maro screams.

Maro doesn't stop screaming until after the constable finds her in the corner of the room, still clutching Father's cane. She doesn't say a word when they lead her to the station and Father's body gets transferred to a nearby town for autopsy. At least that's what the constable tells her when he drives her back home two days later. Maro remembers none of it, only the glint of ghostly needles and the killing pierce. A 'cardiac arrest', the coroner called it. But Maro knows what happened. And she knows why.

What she doesn't know is how to live with it.

Will she share Mother's fate now? Truth is a terrible cross to bear. Mother made her choice, and faced the consequences. When Yaya discovered the truth, she took matters into her own ghostly hands. What is *she* supposed to do now?

She sniffles and the constable asks her if she'll be okay. She nods. It's a lie. He believes her. He leaves.

She trudges uphill on wet ground after the afternoon drizzle. She keeps her eyes on her muddied sneakers and her ears on the slosh her wet socks make at every step. Her heart dreads entering a ghost-filled house. Worse, a house empty of ghosts. Halfway up the hill, she turns left and heads toward the church.

She mouses her way into the shadows of the narthex, then slides into an empty spot by the left wall, at the women's stacidia. She keeps her gaze on her feet, avoiding a single glance towards the right wall of the church—the men's half, where the cantors sit by the episcopal throne, and see Father's seat empty. Murmurs reach her ears: gossip about her unkempt hair, her wrinkled clothes and her muddy shoes. She clenches her fists until her badly-trimmed nails bite into her palms, until the cantor starts a new hymn. Her head snaps up.

Kassiani's Hymn, written for '*the woman befallen on many sins*'. Her hands grasp the armrests and she bites her tongue. Father's favorite. Chanting of wicked women. Did he think her one of them, too? Were they all unworthy of affection, pests deserving only his contempt? *Of his cane?*

Whispers and nudges and muffled voices all around taint the cantor's voice. She follows the others' stares.

Zoe stands at the church's entrance, clad in a simple brown dress, her shoulders straight, her hands clutching her purse a little too tight. But she doesn't look away, and stares everyone down in turn. She has heard. She knows. She *must* know he's dead, as well as how much this evening's mass meant to him. When her eyes meet with Maro's, Maro looks away.

But how much does Zoe know? How much do her broken pieces remember from the night Father died? Did her spirit see Maro in the corner, the screaming, slobbering mess cowering away from

Father's cane, keeping her silence and her distance? Has she come demanding another apology and another admission?

It would be easy, keeping her gaze on her feet and pretend she's a speck of dust beneath the pews. Easier yet, to release the howl that's choking her, and curse the newcomer for ruining Father's final hours. But that wouldn't bring Father back. Father's not coming back. Neither is his scorn, nor his cane. She is free, at last. Yaya made sure of it.

Now does Maro look up, her eyes misty. Through the mist, her path beckons in the candlelight—a path of tears and thorns and knitting needles, their clickity-clack echoing in the distance. But this Via Dolorosa bends in strange angles within the church, past ghost-infested dwellings, through the nymphs' woods, and stretches towards that unfathomable dawn when the sum of broken parts becomes whole again. Atop the episcopal throne, between human and divine justice, the Ferryman holds out his skeletal hand, palm up. Is it the fare he requests, to take her to the end of her journey? Or a toll, to let her through to new, uncharted paths?

Her first step is slow, shy, skittish. What if Charon finds her wanting? But she pushes on, the sloshing of soaked shoes echoing disrespectful in the silence.

"She's going to slap the slut," Martha whispers a little too loud.

Maro stops. Her vertebrae grind as she straightens her back and meets the hateful woman's smirking face.

"Just shut up, already." The words leave her lips sharp as daggers through the chilly air heavy with frankincense. Or, perhaps, as needles.

Martha gasps. Let her gasp and clasp her chest. Let her hate, let her gossip and spew venom. Let her kind keep their silence, until a greater hand sews their lips shut. Maro has carried the sins of her father long enough, and so has Zoe. There's only one path left now, and her feet leave wet marks on the stone floor as she trudges on.

There's a collective gasp when she pulls Zoe in her arms for a late-hour embrace. When Zoe returns the hug, Maro's sobs rob her of voice and her gaze seeks the dark figure upon the throne.

The skeletal palm closes. The hooded head nods. Maro takes Zoe's hand and they both walk out, into a night pregnant with Spring. Beneath their feet, the *Via Dolorosa* stretches open past the pain and the suffering, past the Resurrection and back into life.

See Christine Lucas's story "Via Dolorosa" online at Metaphorosis.
If you liked it, leave a comment. Authors love that!
Remember to subscribe to our e-mail updates so you'll know when new stories are posted.

About the story

"Via Dolorosa" is a story in a series of stories dealing with the Unseen. In my worldview, the Unseen includes elements from the speculatively obvious, that most people cannot see (ghosts, undead, mythic creatures) along with everything a lot of people choose not to see, like abuse.

It also draws a lot from personal experience, from growing up in a household with a Greek small-town mindset, much like the one described in the story. It took me close to four decades and the rise of the Internet to finally accept that it's not okay for a parent to hit their child with their cane or their leather belt, it's not okay to be catcalled or groped at thirteen years old for wearing shorts during an August heatwave, it's never okay to blame the victim, and it's never okay to remain silent when speaking up might change a life.

And last but not least, another point of inspiration for this story (and the others like it) is how the Old Ways were never fully eradicated, despite the efforts of the Christian Church. Their echoes remain in many aspects of everyday life, from common sayings to holidays customs to funerary rites, and mingle with the new ways to create something bigger than both.

A question for the author

Q: What's your favorite *non*-SFF book?

A: *The Mirror Crack'd* by Agatha Christie. I first read it when I was about twelve years old--a cheap, tattered paperback I found in a cardboard box in storage. Despite its problems reflecting the era it was written in, to me it was a revelation: women, in their old age, didn't have to sit around knitting socks and doing housework (unless they wanted to); they could solve mysteries, or even write stories.

About the author

Christine Lucas lives in Greece with her husband and a horde of spoiled animals. A retired Air Force officer and mostly self-taught in English, she was a finalist for the 2017 WSFA award.

werecat99.wordpress.com

A Time for Understanding

Lisa Fox

I lay your bulky, yellow head on my lap, your labored breaths hot against my nightdress. Your massive Labrador paws thrash against an unrelenting hardwood floor, as if you're trying to run to a place without pain. I press my cheek into your soft fur; it cushions the fear that strikes with each violent spasm that threatens to take you from me. I pull you close, wrapping myself around you until the yelps subside to whimpers. Your body shudders. You exhale, deep and deliberate, pushing out the hurt. Your body calms. It is quiet.

I lean back against the cold wall, the chill a respite from the icy-hot adrenaline that pulled me from my dreams to your side. I pet you with long, careful strokes. Your muscles twitch beneath my fingers. A plume of your fur, like dust, hovers above my touch.

As the moon through the bay window bathes us in a ghostly light, I watch you breathe.

I will myself to linger in this moment, to relish the warmth of you.

I run my fingers over your ears and down your neck. I kiss your nose. Still wet.

You offer a single tail thump in thanks.

We huddle together until dawn. I'm grateful for another sunrise.

I can't lose you. I won't lose you. You're everything to me.

We leave for town early. It's a snowy Saturday morning and the village bustles with shoppers; their mittened hands grasp plastic bags bulging with toys and sweaters and trinkets from the Five and Dime. A couple argues as they struggle to tie a freshly cut balsam fir to the top of a red Volkswagen Beetle. A weary mother balances a crying toddler with a grocery bag as a young child skips around her, catching snowflakes on his tongue. You stop to say hello and wag as he gives you a friendly pet. The mother yanks him away, and he cries, his cheeks red with cold and tears.

It's funny how people choose to carry their burdens. Some wear them boldly, like a red knitted scarf on an overcoat. Others bundle them deep within their layers, keeping them close to the heart as they go about their everyday lives. You and I, we blend into the wintry landscape – young woman, old dog, out for a stroll in the snow.

"Almost there, Cody." I graze the top of your head with my fingertips as we tread gingerly across the salted sidewalk. We skirt the ice patches and slush missed in careless tosses of crystal rock. I sense your insecurity with each step. I slow my pace, our gaits parallel.

Marco's Marvelous Pets is on the first floor of a two-story brick building that has stood on the corner of Main and Fifth for over a hundred years. Though time has dulled the structure to the color of cardboard, the window display glows with life. Across the generations, passersby have been drawn to the den of misfit puppies romping in the storefront; litters born to strays on the street, small miracles the world never intended. Children press their palms and foreheads against the glass, hoping for a closer look.

When I was really little and *seen but not heard*, Mother would let us stop for a minute to watch the puppies play while we ran errands. Mother called it the Canine Circus. One by one we'd name the pups – Master and Lion and Clown. She never smiled much, but I remember the way her eyes shone in the reflection of the glass, like some kind of magic trying to break through her frown. Each time, I begged her for a puppy and each time she said no, the moment lost as she tugged me away from the window.

But on my twelfth birthday, my dad brought me to Marco's to choose my puppy. Instead, you chose me.

Barreling out of the kennel, you tripped as you galloped, knocking past Dad and sliding into a display of rawhides. You were as gangly and awkward as I was. My braces and bad perm were a perfect match for your oversized paws and lolling tongue. You wiggled out from under the mountain of bones and leapt to greet me. Bouncing off my kneecaps, you knocked me to the floor and buried me in barrage of puppy kisses.

From that moment on, I was your person.

We huddle under the awning to shield ourselves from the snow. I stomp ice cakes from my boots. You wiggle and shimmy to free yourself from the frigid wetness, too weak for a glorious full shake. I brush the snow from your back and open the icy glass door. The metal of the handle tingles my skin, sending a slight shock through my bare hands. Together, we enter the shop, and its warmth embraces us.

Francis Marco IV is the current proprietor. Shriveled and gaunt, with a complexion like paste, he may be the oldest man I have ever seen. A cloud of cottony hair encircles his scalp, and a faded grey sweater hangs from his diminutive frame as if it were intended for a more robust man. Deep wrinkles form rivulets down his cheeks and around his eyes. He looks at us through thick, horn-rimmed glasses; his deep-set blue eyes belie his age. Marco shuffles loafered feet across the worn floor, a weathered wooden cane supporting his weight in one hand; a bag of Puppy Chow in the other.

Your nose twitches and you sneeze. The smell of must, wet dog, and slush clings to the wood-paneled walls. I adjust my eyes; flickering fluorescent bulbs buzz overhead. The store is crowded with pet supplies, but absent customers.

Stacks of silver dishes, walls of rawhides, a fortress of sheepskin beds pile almost to the ceiling. Despite the retail disarray, I've always been able to find just the item I'm looking for, as if it's risen through the mess just for me. There's always been something special about the things that Marco sells. With a box of his dog biscuits, even the unruliest dog behaves. Marco's chew toys make a dog forget the temptations of wayward shoes and children's homework. And one drop of Marco's Special Salve heals even the ugliest of ear infections.

The magic pill we're looking for must be hiding somewhere on these cluttered shelves.

Eyes focused intently on Marco, you attempt to sit, as if on command. Painstakingly, you lower your hind quarters to the ground. You wince as your tail approaches the floor. "Good boy," I say, scratching the soft fur behind your ears.

"Nice old dog you have there," Marco says.

You bark once, as if in agreement.

Marco chuckles, his throaty laugh almost too strong for someone of his stature. "Age hasn't robbed him of his personality." He leans in, peering from you, back to me, as if examining us. "Been a long time since I've seen you."

I pause, caught under an embarrassed spotlight. I've been purchasing Cody's food and toys online for years. It *has* been a long time since I've been to Marco's.

"We haven't been out much, other than to go to the vet." I frown. "We've been to every one in the county. But no one has been able to help."

Marco's eyes take in your expanded girth, the hot spot growing from your right paw, your hind legs trembling with the pressure of sitting. You return his gaze, tilting your head slightly. Something about Marco amuses you.

"What makes you think we'll have anything helpful here?"

"Well, I just thought … you always seem to have just what Cody needs, whenever he needs it."

"Oh?" His eyes widen.

"Maybe a special kind of treatment? Something...holistic...that the vets wouldn't consider?"

Marco chuckles. He rests his skeletal, liver spotted hand on your head. You turn to lick it as he whispers to you, "How silly. She thinks I'm some sort of old shaman for dogs."

"I didn't mean it that way." I kick at the floor with the toe of my wet boot.

Why should I think this small-town pet shop owner could provide an answer that so many doctors couldn't? Desperation is the enemy of logic, and although I learned at an early age that doctors were far from godlike, I just needed someone to help me. Even if it was an old man in a musty old shop.

"I'm sorry. It was a stupid question."

He places the Puppy Chow on the scratched Formica counter. The bag crackles as it settles in place. The puppies tussling in the shop window halt their willy-nilly ear-biting play, whimpering at the sound of the bag.

Marco slides his glasses up to the bridge of his nose. His eyes narrow; scrutinizing us. He turns a heavy gaze toward you and back to me, where it rests uncomfortably. "I have what you need," Marco says. "If you're willing to trust me."

Trust – that fog-laden bridge between promise and truth, navigated by the very young or the very foolish. I learned to avoid that path long ago. It's like being handed a bouquet of roses and having them wilt in my palms; the last viable bloom reserved for a coffin at a gravesite. Or believing mother's words that she'd always be there, never realizing "there" was on the dirty tile of a bathroom floor, her fingers wrapped around an empty bottle of booze. The surest way to align promise with truth was to bypass bridges, finding my own way with you by my side.

It's impossible to trust anyone.

Your nose twitches as you sniff the air in the direction of the puppy food.

Anyone, except for you.

My father's decline began just before he brought me to you. Not that I recognized it at the time; I was too wrapped up in my own pre-teen priorities. It wasn't until much later, looking back on those photographs of your puppy days, that I saw what wasn't evident to a child's eyes.

Dad's tanned skin, bronzed from years of working in construction, had faded to an ashen pallor. His bright eyes had lost their spark, sunken in behind cheekbones that had become too prominent.

I remember now how his hands shook during those fleeting and frustrating days when we were housetraining you, and the way his pajamas hung from his frame as he tended to your nighttime whimpers. I can still see the tiny bruises on his ankles left by your needle-teeth as you explored the world by mouthing it – I'd always thought it odd how the marks your nibbling left on me were short lived, and with Dad, how they seemed more permanent. But nothing was permanent for him, and at the same time, everything was. I suppose it's like that when people reach the end.

Around the time you had grown into your oversized paws, Dad stopped laughing. The sound of him changed. *He's got a cold*, Mother told me. *Chronic bronchitis. It'll go away.* His weight loss was explained as *a much-needed diet to lose that belly of his.* The days and nights he spent on the couch, my mother attributed to a bad economy. *No one builds houses in a recession.* He spent hours in silence, just staring, the TV remote in hand. Tissues piled up and spilled from the tray table to the floor; meals were left untouched and cold.

Mother told me to leave my father alone, to keep "that dog" away from him. She took up residence in the kitchen, chain-smoking until her voice adopted the raspy timbre of a woman twice her age, gin and tonic on the rocks her constant companion.

My dad was dying, and I didn't know.

Maybe I didn't want to know. Maybe I wasn't ready.

At the very end, when machines pushed the air into my father's chest, I spent my days doing homework in the cold antiseptic loneliness of a hospital room. Nurses came to check in, but they said little to me about my dad. They would help with the occasional math problem or pat my head and offer me some Jell-O. As if that would make me feel any better about the alarms that rang off from the machines almost hourly, or the stale, urine-tinged air that made me sneeze.

You were the only thing that made me feel better. Rolling together in the cool grass as we picked you up from the neighbor's house, your muddy paws on my shoulders were as strong as any hug. I didn't even flinch when the neighbor yelled at me and demanded my chore money because you'd dug through her gardenias. She called you a naughty puppy, but I knew better. Flowers could be replanted, but you, you were a good puppy.

I wished I had been able to bring you with me on those long days I spent at my Dad's side. Your nose, working hard to find him hiding deep in his work boots or tucked away under the knitted afghan on the couch, told me how much you missed him. I pictured you on my lap, nudging my hand to be petted as I sat for all those hours on that lumpy pleather hospital chair. The nurses would have brought you cookies – the good stuff – with some extra for me. Dad would have been happy to have you there, even though those machines kept him from saying anything at all.

I thought about that a lot, and one day, I suggested to Mother that we sneak you in to see him. *My backpack's big enough*, I said, stowing you inside. You whimpered and scratched at the canvas until I unzipped the bag just enough for you to poke your head out and lick my cheek.

Mother just shook her head at me. She did that often, especially when I asked her if my Dad was going to get any better. And when he'd come home. When life would go back to normal.

She refused to tell me anything. She answered every question with *He'll be fine. Trust me.*

Mother sent me home from the hospital early one cloudy Saturday afternoon. You and I had run around the yard most of the day, playing soccer, until the rains came, and we huddled together on the couch. We watched movies and ate popcorn. Doing nothing special was what made it special. It felt good to snuggle with you, lay my cheek against your head, feel the familiar for just a little while.

Dad died that night, just about the time I was brushing my teeth. I was thinking about how good I would look when my braces finally came off as my dad fought against his final breath, alone. Mother called me from the local pub to tell me the news.

I never said goodbye.

Marco removes his glasses. Reaching over the countertop, he places a hand on my arm. A feather pokes out from the fabric of my down jacket, grazing his skin.

"I'd like to help you, Allison. But I need you to do something first."

I nod, feeling my brows furrow.

"I'd like you to take a good look at your dog."

You yawn and slide to the floor with a thud, laying your nose between your front paws. You fight the gravity and fatigue that weigh upon your eyelids. With a soft snore, you surrender to your nap.

"I'm looking at him," I say. I wonder what point Marco is trying to make. "He's tired. He's an old dog." I feign a smile. "Just like you said."

"What is he telling you?"

"Telling me? I'm not sure I understand." Awkwardly, I wriggle away from the old man's touch. Gooseflesh fights the layers of my winter clothing, leaving my skin cold. "How can he tell me anything? He's a dog. Last time I checked, they don't talk."

"He'll tell you what he needs, if you are open to it." Marco leans on his cane. He purses his lips and stares at me – through me – as if he's trying to read my thoughts.

I hold my breath to fight the sigh – or is it a laugh? – that threatens to push through and wonder if Marco is just a lonely old man desperate for company. Or maybe he's senile. It's the only explanation for why he continues to speak nonsensically instead of doing something to help you, as he said he could. My gaze rests on the merchandise surrounding us. I need Marco to stop talking and hand me that wondrous potion, that rare salve or special bandage that we came here for.

I glance at you. Our time together is finite. I feel its tug with each passing minute.

Marco shifts his weight and appears to sink further into his sweater. "What you need, what he needs, is right here, just as it's always been," he says. "If you're not afraid to find it."

He fixes his gaze upon you; you raise your head, open your eyes, and blink. Twice.

"Why would I be afraid to help my dog?" I'm tiring of Marco's word games. And there's something about his countenance that burrows into me like a determined tick. Old people seem to think that wisdom is built by the number of footprints they leave on the earth. But the truth is, it's the weight of the imprints that matters most. And how well they withstand the tide. Francis Marco IV doesn't understand me at all.

"Fear distorts our judgment, my dear. It is the thief of faith."

You lay quietly at my feet. Fully awake, your knowing eyes shift from me, to this frail man who speaks in riddles, and back to me again.

"I've been all over creation trying to find something that will help cure Cody." The walls of useless pet goods are suddenly stifling. "What he needs has nothing to do with fear. Or faith."

"The time for cure has passed. He needs something more." Marco picks up the Puppy Chow and resumes his scuffing walk, turning his back to us. The patter of dry food pelts off the metal trough. The sound of the puppies' crunching fills the silence.

Heat spreads across my cheeks. Marco's speculative nonsense is wasting valuable moments that could be spent seeking a solution. I grab your leash with both hands, tight, to stop them from shaking. This man is no better than the veterinarian who handed me a pamphlet with that ridiculous poem about rainbows. Or that neighbor who told me, as I cried at my Dad's casket, he was in a better place now. Unfulfilled promises of help, empty words, they leave me with nothing but hopelessness. Tears threaten as I tug on your leash, imploring you to rise on tired legs.

"I'm sorry we came here. Let's go, Cody."

Marco peers over his shoulder and smiles. "Please don't leave. I've been expecting you for a while, now, Allison."

I lean down and wrap my arms around your middle, desperate to pull you up and get out of this place. You won't budge. *I may have to carry you*, I think.

Breathless with the fruitless effort of moving you, I stand. You look up at me apologetically. I cross my arms and glare at Marco. "Why would you expect me, when I haven't been here in years?"

Marco turns away, ignoring my question. He dangles a smooth hand into the puppy den. A fluffy brown dog toddles toward him, sniffs Marco's flesh and opens her tiny mouth wide. She nibbles Marco's index finger like it's rawhide. You bark and thump your tail, your curiosity piqued by this small creature as much as mine is by the man who feeds him.

The puppy enjoys a final taste and, abandoning Marco's hand, wiggles her way back in through the pack, nose first, to her dinner. Marco retrieves his cane and limps toward the front door.

"They always come back, when it's time," he murmurs. His reflection in the glass glows an icy fluorescence as Marco turns the lock and flips the sign to *Closed*.

"What are you doing?" I ask, my voice quavering.

Slow-motion panic percolates within me; legs poised to run, feet rooted to the fading tile. Then adrenaline overwhelms like a winter squall. I lift you as high as I can off the floor. Feet scrambling, you writhe for freedom. I fall back, cushioning your body as we crash to the ground, trapped with this strange old man.

Marco leans in. The glasses that rest halfway down the bridge of his nose magnify his eyes; his pupils an eclipse that demands my gaze.

"Helping Cody. Helping you." His voice is a whisper. "Your father came here because he knew you'd need someone very special to love after he was gone." He bends slowly toward the floor, aged knees creaking with effort. His outstretched palm strokes your head. Your ears flutter, as if lifted by a breeze.

"Cody was his final gift to you."

"We've always been together," I whisper. "I can't lose him, too."

You stretch your neck and close your eyes as Marco's hand runs over your fur, his caress so light it seems as if he's not touching you at all. And I recall the days, months, and years after my Dad died, when you lay, warm next to me, as I sobbed into my pillow. The sunsets we watched together on the front stoop, my arm draped around you, as summer faded with the turning of leaves. How you wagged and wiggled, greeting me as I returned from school to an empty house. How your head tilted with interest, as I read you my salutatory address before graduation, knowing you'd listen when Mother would not. The way you held your head out the window, as if defying the wind, as you sat in the front seat of my car when I first got my license. Waiting for your treat outside the bank as I cashed my first paycheck. Munching on cardboard boxes as I moved us into our apartment.

Sadness and fear converge and morph to tears that threaten to fall from a precipice I've hidden behind years of resolve. After my Dad died, there was no knight to rescue me from the tower of bad dreams; no healer to kiss away the pain of skinned knees or broken hearts. I grew up lonely as an orphan. You were my family, my friend. My only joy.

"Your father's love for you flows through Cody." Marco inches upright, two hands grasping the curve of his cane to support the weight of his timeworn body. "It's everything you know. It's part of who you are. But it is time for understanding, now." He taps the cane on the floor for emphasis. "It is time to listen to Cody."

"But that's impossible." This is a place I am not ready to visit, an indulgence I'm unwilling to grant to this stranger who knows too much.

This stranger who has shown more interest in us than any other human has, in a very long time.

Marco removes his glasses. He stares at me with wide eyes. "We cannot see love with our eyes, Allison. But does that mean it does not exist? That it is impossible?"

I shake my head, my throat dry.

You emit a whining, yearning bark and swat a beefy paw at me, batting it against my leg. An invitation. The eagerness of puppyhood glimmers behind your old-dog eyes.

"I'll be waiting." Marco looks at you, laying loyal at my side. "Whenever you're ready to listen."

Marco turns and shuffles toward the back of the store. Together, we watch him stroll down an aisle that seems to lengthen with each labored step, his form shrinking until he vanishes into the stacks of pet supplies.

"Come on, old friend," I say. You push forward off your hind legs. Your limbs quiver and bow, failing as gravity grasps with a cruel hand. I bend next to you; I feel your hot breath on my cheek and smell the acrid scent of illness rising from within you. You pant rhythmically; your soft brown eyes imploring my assistance in an embarrassed silence.

"It's ok, buddy." I crouch down and wrap my arms around your middle. Gently, I pull you upright. Your front legs flail beneath you as you scramble to regain your footing. "I have you. I won't let you fall." Your tail twitches in thanks.

We haven't much time. Words alone will not heal you. Whether it's medicine or magic or some impossible miracle cure, I need to keep searching for an answer not to be found in a small-town pet shop. Time was a steep price for this fool's errand.

I tug your leash in the direction of the exit. "Come on, Cody. We've got to keep trying." You stop, four paws planted to the linoleum. Your legs are rigid, feet dug in firmly. Your tail extends in perfect parallel to the floor. Like a chiseled marble statue, you stand immobile, unmalleable, and defiant.

"Come on, boy." I pull again, more emphatically. You whine and sniff the air in the direction of Marco's departure. I squat down and lay my head on yours. "We're going to find someone who can help you." Your ears pull pack and your nose twitches.

I stand. You sit.

Woof.

You bark with a resolve I haven't heard in a long time, with the same determination you showed on a day long ago, when you'd found a burrow of baby bunnies in our yard. You stood over them, rooted and protecting them, taking kicks from Mother's landscaper as he tried to push you away. *He's trying to tell us something!* I'd shouted.

Those bunnies lived because I listened to you. And because you didn't give up on them.

Woof.

Are you trying to tell me something now?

I shake my head. That old man's gotten to me. If I'm not careful, I'll start speaking in riddles, too.

"I must be losing my mind. Time to go."

Woof.

Desperation *is* the enemy of logic, but this shop, this old man – they've been anything but logical. And despite the exasperating poetic conversations and odd platitudes harnessing us since we entered the store, I know we're just about out of options.

We've come this far. Might as well see it through – whatever it is.

"Okay, Cody," I say, once again helping you to stand. "Let's go find Mr. Marco. You lead the way."

As we work our way down the aisle in the direction of Marco, a stray red rubber ball falls from a crowded shelf, bounces, and rolls to a stop in front of us – as if the store is beckoning you to play. You push at it with your nose.

"Want this?" I ask.

You lick your chops in affirmation – in *anticipation*? I shake my head and retrieve the toy. We continue toward a narrow hallway at the back of the shop. Worn brown paneling buckles toward us; the walls push further inward with each step we take. My shoulder scrapes the warping wood as we reach a door at the end.

You stand stoic, watching me. "Ready?" I ask you. But for what, I'm not sure.

I crouch down until we are at eye level. I extend a hand to you, open-palmed. You take hesitant steps forward, just as you did the day we brought you home and you first walked into our kitchen, overwhelmed by the cacophony of foreign smells and sights. You lick my wrist, the warm flesh of your pink tongue easing the drumbeat of my pulse.

Woof. Your tail wags side to side, increasing its rhythmic tempo.

The door creaks open, releasing a burst of frigid air from within. I'm met with a chill I've never felt before as Marco waves us inside a small, windowless room the size of a storage closet. Except for two metal folding chairs, the room is empty. A lone lightbulb hangs from the ceiling, its pull-string sways gently above us. Marco shuffles toward me and places a metal dog whistle in my hand. *Another of Marco's marvelous pet supplies.* My palm tingles; it's as cold as ice.

"Please, sit." He gestures toward a chair. As I wonder what we're doing in this odd little room, and why I decided to stay, I obey.

He takes your leash and pets your head. Together you take a few steps toward the wall opposite me; your tail is raised, your gait peppier than I've seen in years. He settles you into a *down* position. Your descent is slow but easy. Paws forward, head erect, you stare at me, eyes wide. As you pant, you look like you're smiling.

Marco shuffles toward the empty seat. He leans on his cane for support as he lowers himself.

"When you are ready, blow into the whistle."

I nod at the old man and cough to stifle the laugh that bubbles in my throat. Perhaps it's the solemnity with which Marco handed me the dog whistle, or simply the tickle of nerves in my belly, desperate for release. Either way, I feel a full-on belly laugh threatening – an urge as strong and inappropriate as a scream on a cross-country flight.

That is, until I look at you.

You lay your head down on your paws, nose twitching, tail thumping. Waiting, like you used to wait next to your supper dish, back in the days when dinner was more than just a necessity for you, it was an event.

I take a deep breath as I raise the whistle to my lips. I blow out, hard. A tinny screeching pierces my eardrums. I grab for my ears and drop the whistle. It clatters to the floor and transforms from silver to a brilliant white; bright light bursts from within it. The room dissolves around us – walls, ceiling, and floor morphing until they're indistinguishable. I squeeze my eyes against the light as I fall. An icy tingling enshrouds me; it hurts as it soothes.

Voices vibrate above, below, and around me. I crack open my eyelids and hold my hands up, seeing only a faint outline of myself, like a child's chalk drawing before it is brushed away by time. I am suspended in space, in non-space. I feel your presence. I sense Marco is near.

And then I see you. You're like a hearth ember floating through the mist, feather-light, *down, down, down*. We hover side by side and land together in a cloud that's as soft as your angel fur.

"Allison? Allison?"

A voice. *Cody?*

Your words burst in a staccato outpouring of discovery. Your speech sets fire to logic.

"Allison! Why are you lying down?" You nudge me with your nose, slipping your head beneath my arm. "Time to get up! It's time to play!" Your voice is gravelly, like that of an old man – poignantly misaligned with the vibrant, wiggling dog nuzzling into me.

I pause, not quite knowing how to engage in an impossible conversation. With my dog.

You tug my sleeve so hard I almost fall over. I can't remember the last time I've seen you this animated. Your nose is cold; it tickles my skin. "Okay, Cody. I'd love to play."

It really *is* him. The puppy of my youth.

"Allison? Do you have that ball?"

It *was* an invitation.

"I do."

"Yippie!" You leap straight up, pitching forward into a somersault. "Lemme have it. Lemme have it!"

I reach out and catch you; you're light as air in my arms. I stroke your head; your tail beats against my thighs. Your panting intensifies. "Take it easy, Codybear. That was quite a flip." I feel your chest tense as you breathe in. "How are you feeling?"

You pause. All your life, you've been asked what you need. Dinner? A walk? But never how you feel.

"Allison, I feel ... funny. But not ha-ha funny like when you laugh. I like it when you laugh, Allison."

Sometimes it's the wonder of the little things we do, the things we don't notice ourselves, that makes all the difference. Like the way my father fluffed out the morning paper while he had his coffee, insisting that the window stay open just a crack, so he could *feel* the new day. Or the way he'd chuckle as he read me the Sunday Funny Pages.

For all these years, you've watched my every move, heard every sound, perhaps memorized every gesture. Just as I did with my Dad.

"Allison, when can we play? I want to play. It's all white in here – like snow! Let's run!"

You wriggle in my arms and stop, wincing. I feel your low whine quaver against me.

I stroke your back to calm you. "Remember our first winter? We had so much fun."

"You called me your little snow dog."

I smile. "Remember I brought you a top hat, a scarf, and even a carrot for a nose?"

"I ate the carrot. It was crunchy."

"That was a long time ago, Cody."

You pause, contemplating. "Why don't I run in the snow anymore, Allison?" You look up at me with sad eyes. "I don't really run at all, do I?"

"It's been hard for you, my friend." I recall your tentative, hobbling steps; your nighttime restlessness. "It hurts my heart to see you in pain."

"You hurt, Allison? Maybe you should ask Mr. Marco for a Band-Aid. I promise not to pull it off you."

I stroke your ears and roll the tips between my fingers like I used to when you were a puppy. It was our special signal of quiet time. And now, my time to listen.

"There's a lot we need to talk about, Cody."

"It's about your shoe, isn't it? I'm sorry. I know it was your favorite. But you weren't home, and it smelled like you. Chewing it made me feel much better."

I exhale slowly to ease the flow of words I'd rather not speak. "Cody, we're here now. Wherever here is. And I've seen you do things I'd never have thought possible." I lower my head and look away from you, into the void. "It's like somehow you've become young again."

"Young, Allison? But I'm an old dog now." You giggle. A dog's giggle. "You're silly, Allison. How can an old dog be young?"

"I don't really know." Silence. You lean into me. Your warmth exudes home.

Marco appears beside me, materializing through the light. His voice is a whisper, a cool, circling breeze.

"Cody, how would you like to go to a place where the sun will always shine upon you? Where you can run and frolic across endless fields, and never tire." He strokes your head. "I can bring you to this place."

I bite my lip and turn away, closing my eyes to squeeze away the tears before you see them fall. You deserve this life – the effortless existence I always hoped my father had found.

"Allison! That sound like fun! Like old times. Let's go, let's go, let's go!"

I remember the sound of your nails tap-tap-tapping on the hardwood of my dining room, how you held your blue leash between your teeth, letting it hang down as you waited for me to grasp the end. The whole-body wiggle of joy I never thought I'd see again.

"Cody." I sigh. "I can't come with you."

Your tail droops. You whimper. I'm reminded of that first night when my home became yours, the sad cries subsiding only when I invited you to snuggle in the warmth of my bed. Until that day, I never knew puppies cried.

"Cody?"

"Allison, I don't want to go without you. Mr. Marco can keep his sunshine and his fields."

I shake my head and try to resist the knot twisting in my throat. The ice engulfing us does little to dull the pain. I'm watching. I'm listening. And you've been holding on, so hard, for me. As I know my father tried to, for as long as he could.

How difficult must it have been for my dad to lift a hammer and drive each nail into your doghouse? The weight of a paintbrush like an anvil with his every brushstroke, knowing that this would be his final creation? Yet each day, we worked together until the evening sky turned pink and the cicadas serenaded us; a small, active puppy curled up at our feet to snooze in the grass. Dad and I speculated on the many adventures you and I would have together. Halloweens spent in matching human and canine superhero costumes. The excitement of Christmas morning – you, tearing through a pile of presents seeking a bone wrapped up just for you, complete with a bow. Future memories my father designed but would never build. The foundation of my life lived without him.

I look to Marco. We lock eyes. In this moment, I see. I hear. I understand. The past, present, and future converge in Marco's gaze, and I realize that we're standing at the foot of a bridge to a place I stopped believing in a long time ago. I grasp the peace that has eluded me for years; it's woven like silk through my fingers as I reach out and run my hands through your fur.

And I hear my words echo before they leave my mouth.

"Cody. My dad will be there, waiting for you."

Your ears perk up, your head tilts slightly to the right with interest. *My Dad.* One of your favorite phrases. And after all these years, his imprint remains strong. He's still one of the people you cherish the most.

"Do you remember when you were a puppy, my Dad used to nap with you, outside in the sun?" I recall the image of you – wiggling as you dropped a ball at my father's feet, nuzzling his hand, determined to play. But my dad's hand lay limp and useless beside him. He had only the strength to brush his fingertips down your side.

"How far is this place? I'm tired, Allison. What if I fall down?"

"I will never let you fall."

I lean down and lay my head atop yours, wrapping my arms around you. I inhale the sweetness of you – fresh snow and summertime and falling leaves and newly-cut grass – and allow the tears to wash over the precipice of my grief and into your soft fur.

"Cody, it's okay for you to go." I breathe in, deep staccato. For your heart to flourish, I know that mine must break. "Run free, my friend. Goodbye."

Goodbye. A word that stops time. I wasn't ready then. I'm not ready now. I clutch you tighter, willing the light to linger as I absorb the last vestiges of your warmth. You turn, nose pressed to my eyelids, sniffing out my sadness. A final kiss.

I'm sprawled on the floor of the dimly lit storage room. Ice crystals cling to my drenched hair and clothing. My face has lost all feeling.

You are gone.

Marco shuffles over and takes your leash from his back pocket.

"Time is finite." Marco's whisper is soft as cashmere. "But for just a moment, I can offer you a glimpse.

"A glimpse?" I sit up, holding my head.

Marco touches my wrist, bringing my hands down to my lap. He places your worn Nylon collar in my hands and retrieves the dog whistle from his pocket. He blows into it gently, silently, producing a small cloud. In the mist, I behold an emerald field, an azure cloudless sky and you, Cody – strong in the innocent determination of your puppyhood. You bound effortlessly, intently, despite oversized paws that threaten to trip you in a roly-poly bliss. You run free, determined to catch the rubber ball that sails like a red comet through the pristine sky.

The red rubber ball tossed effortlessly by my father.

I trudge toward the exit of Marco's Marvelous Pets. Wiping my cheeks with the back of my hand, I wonder what the world will look like when I walk through those doors. If time will stop, if the clocks will keep ticking. If everything will be different. Or if it will all be the same, and it's just me who will be different. Will others know what I've seen? What I've done? Will they even care?

"Wait, please," Marco says, shuffling toward the puppy den. He lifts a fluffy brown dog and offers me the squirming bundle. "This puppy needs a home."

He places her into my arms. Small paws bat at my long, loose hair as she wriggles in my embrace.

I observe her wide eyes staring at me, the way her brows lift in the wonder of a new human. I snuggle her close.

She will never be you, Cody.

But she needs a home. And I need a friend.

"How much does she cost?"

"What is the price of faith?" Marco smiles and turns from me, moving once again toward the back of the store.

"Faith," I say. The puppy yaps in reply. "It's got a nice ring to it."

See Lisa Fox's story "A Time for Understanding" online at Metaphorosis.
If you liked it, leave a comment. Authors love that!
Remember to subscribe to our e-mail updates so you'll know when new stories are posted.

About the story

This story is a deeply personal one. I originally wrote this as a 1,000 word flash fiction piece four days before my mother died. She'd been in the hospital for weeks, declining steadily, though we had no idea why.

Her last days were spent on a bi-pap breathing machine - the mask was basically keeping her alive - and I never really got the chance to talk to her about what she wanted, I never really got to say goodbye. The decision to take her off the machine was mine to make.

The "what if" here for me was this: what if we actually have the chance to say goodbye to our loved ones, under impossible circumstances? What would we talk about? What would we do?

In writing this piece, I thought about my mom and what we went through with her. I also thought about my real-life Cody- my first furbaby- and what it would have been like to be able to say goodbye to him at the end. And the idea was born.

It's funny how life works. It took me a long time to get this story just right, to come to terms with my main character's journey and what I was really trying to say. And as I was in the final stages of editing the piece with *Metaphorosis*, my father passed away. It was very different than what I went through with my mom, and honestly the type of passing my MC had hoped for with her own dad. Oddly enough, I thought about my MC and her lack of closure with her father when I made the decision to let my two boys into the hospital to see my dad one last time. Our own lives often give birth to our fiction, yet sometimes our fiction serves to teach us lessons we didn't know we needed.

A question for the author

Q: Do you often include animals in your stories? What role do they play?

A: It's funny, although animals (particularly dogs) have always played a huge role in my life, I usually don't include them in my work. That's not to say I won't do so in the future.

Aside from "A Time For Understanding," I did write (and was fortunate enough to publish) a flash fiction piece- political satire- about a healthcare system that proposed using dogs as doulas to save costs on childbirth for the uninsured. It's a crazy and bizarre story; the comfort my yellow lab (my real-life Cody) provided me during my two pregnancies - especially when I was on bed rest with my first - was an inspiration. And back in high school, I wrote a short story about how it felt to say goodbye to our 17 year-old poodle. It was riddled with teen angst but the sentiment was certainly there- it was a story I needed to write at the time.

I think animals serve so many different roles for us in life and I am personally convinced that that "one special dog" is the one waiting, tail wagging, to bring us to the other side when we pass on. Maybe I should write more about animals...

About the author

Lisa Fox is a pharmaceutical market researcher by day and fiction writer by night. She enjoys crafting short stories and short screenplays across genres, but her passion is for Speculative Fiction/Drama hybrids. She thrives on the thrill of creating something out of nothing, in transforming life's 'what ifs' to prose that flashes a mirror on the human condition. As a writer, nothing makes her happier than having readers say her work made them feel something or look at the world in a different way.

Lisa has been writing since childhood, but took a too-long hiatus from the creative world after graduating from college when the responsibilities of work and family took precedence. She started writing again just over three years ago and likens it to getting back together with an old friend.

A resident of northern New Jersey, USA, Lisa relishes the chaos of everyday suburban life. She and her husband Dan are kept busy by the comings and goings of their two sons, ages 14 and 10, and by the demands of their couch-dwelling golden retriever. Lisa hopes to begin working on a novel in the foreseeable future — she just needs to get those first few words on the page.

lisafoxiswriting.wordpress.com, @iamlisafox10800

Fur and Feathers

Jess Koch

Dad was the first in our family to change. It was slow in the beginning: one morning he woke to find the skin on the back of his hand had hardened and darkened overnight. When I asked about it, he told me it was just dry skin, and I believed him because I was only twelve at the time and didn't know what I know now.

As weeks passed, the dark patch grew. It spread up his arm, across his chest, climbing over his collarbones and up his neck. He tried to hide it under heavy layers of clothes, but I noticed other changes too: his movement was slower and stiffer than before, and his arms grew so long that his fingers could nearly touch the floor when he was standing up. His legs changed too, widening and beginning to curve outward at his knees.

Late at night I could hear his bones creaking like a tree in a storm.

My twin sister Becca said it first: "It's the change." She whispered it to me while we lay in our room, our breaths close and our fingers tangled like branches underneath the protective blanket fort that Mom had helped us build earlier in the day.

"Like the guy in the woods?" I asked, recalling the man from the spring before.

She nodded, her face only illuminated by a yellow lamp glow diffused by the sheets.

"Are you scared?"

She kept nodding.

"Me too."

She squeezed my hands even tighter and we fell asleep holding onto each other.

Growths sprouted from Dad's arms that budded with small green pods, unfurling into baby leaves which he tugged out like weeds until his fingers became so stiff that he could no longer bend them. After that, Becca and I would sit with him every night, pulling the pods out with our nimble fingers because he said it might help stop the change. And as we did so, he would try to peel the bark from his skin, spilling blood onto the living room floor.

But every morning there were more green buds than we had pulled the night before and the bark grew back over his raw skin, harder and darker. I asked him if the changes hurt and he said "No, Little Bird."

Mom was quiet during his change. She wouldn't pluck the leaves or cut away the bark like Dad asked her to. I would go to her, crying, and show her handfuls of baby leaves curled up in my palms like dead moths, and she would take them from me and bury them in the garden.

I heard them arguing, late one night when I couldn't fall asleep. I got up and tip-toed down to their room and pressed my ear against their door.

"No," I heard Dad say.

"There's a spot by the garden—" Mom said.

"I'm not going to sit outside like a damned animal."

"You can't stay in the house anymore." she said. They were both quiet for a few moments and then Mom said: "I'm so sorry, love."

"Me too," Dad said. "I didn't expect this to happen so quickly."

"It's all right."

"I'm not sure that it is," he said. "I don't know how you can be so hopeful about...about all of this."

"Because we're going be together again someday. All of us. I promise. Can I at least show you the spot in the yard tomorrow?"

"Sure."

And then they were silent.

But by morning, Dad's legs had grown off the bed, becoming roots that dug through the floorboards into the earth beneath the house and he could no longer be moved from the bed. In the days that followed, his arms continued to lengthen, Mom had us open all the windows in their room so they could grow outside of the house.

For many nights after that, while Mom made him soup, because it was the only food he could swallow, Becca and I would climb out onto his branches and pull the little leaves until there were none. But soon his arms split into more branches and those branches split into even more and we could no longer reach all the leaves.

One night, Becca said she didn't want to go into the room anymore because she was scared and because nothing we were doing was working. I went without her. Dad had risen from the bed until his head was nearly touching the ceiling. He couldn't open his eyes anymore, but he always knew it was me.

"Little Bird." His voice was coarse and quiet.

"Hi, Dad."

A small silence followed as I walked toward him.

"Little Bird, where is your sister?"

"She's right here." I lied.

"I love you both."

"We're right here," I said, placing both of my palms on the bark of his trunk.

That was the last night I heard him speak. After that, he rose quickly, up and up, widening as he grew until he broke through the roof. His roots thickened and snaked through the hallways of the house. Bark covered his nose and his mouth until all that remained of him was the outline of his face in the trunk of the tree.

It wasn't until months later, in summer, that Dad's elm finally stopped growing at an unnatural speed. Our little house was in bad shape. Half the roof was gone, the foundation damaged, and most of the rooms overtaken by enormous roots and branches.

A heavy storm passed through in late August and poured rain in through the cracks, and flooded parts of the house. Mom moved another bed into the room I shared with Becca, where the roof was still intact, and the three of us slept there from then on.

Days after the storm, when the flooded lawn had mostly dried up, Mom strung up a tire swing on one of Dad's lower branches for us. She said we should spend time with him, talk to him. He would want to hear us, she said.

"But he's gone," Becca said to me when I climbed onto the top of the tire, with the rope between my legs, and held on tight. "It's just a tree."

I wondered whether Mom or Becca was right. Becca pulled the tire back and let it go, pushing it forward as it swung back.

We were both quiet, looking up as I swung and Becca pushed, watching the elm tree's leaves rustling in the light wind. Mom was on the roof now, repairing the damage by hammering planks around the tree's trunk and patching holes. I hoped Mom was right. I was pretty sure I could feel him still there, like he was standing just behind the tree, watching us.

I noticed Becca had stopped pushing the swing. I looked down to see her staring across the yard at two figures that had emerged from the woods and were walking toward us.

The smaller figure, a little boy who was maybe four or five, started running and stopped a few feet away from the base of the tree that grew out of the side of our house, his head craned backward, his jaw slack.

"Wow," he said in a long breath.

"Jordan, come back here." The other figure, a woman, waved a frantic hand at the boy and he rushed back to her side. As he ran, I noticed that the back of his neck was covered in a slick, black fur. I reached around to the back of my own neck, where my fingers met only soft, naked skin.

Mom stopped hammering when the woman shouted.

"Isn't that..." I started to say.

"Yeah," Becca said.

Mom climbed down the ladder that was propped up against the house and crossed the distance of lawn between her and the visitors.

"Lovely day," the woman said, looking uncomfortable, her gaze flitting between the tree, Becca and I on the swing, and Mom.

"Sure is," Mom said. "It's Kate, right?"

"Yes, Katherine, but...Kate is fine, yes. And this is Jordan."

"Ah, right. Hello Jordan. How are you?"

The little boy burrowed into his mother's shirt.

"Sorry for the intrusion. We were picking mushrooms in the woods and saw the..." She pointed up at the tree. "Is that..."

"My husband, yes."

"I'm so sorry for your loss."

Mom said nothing for a moment, taking off her thick work gloves, and then said: "Thank you Kate, that's very kind."

Kate rubbed her son's back with one hand and tugged at locks of her frizzy red hair with the other. "I was also wondering if...you tried...was there anything that helped?"

"Helped with what?"

"To slow the change."

"No, there was nothing that helped." Mom shifted her eyes to the boy. "Is he changing? Is that why you're asking?"

The woman gaped and pulled the little boy to her belly, covering his ears with her hands. "Don't say that in front of him."

"Doesn't he know what happened to his father? Families tend to change faster after the first. Surely you knew this was a possibility."

"Well, aren't you afraid for yourself? For your daughters?" Kate stared at us, concern carving deep lines across her forehead.

"It's nothing to be afraid of." Mom wiped sweat from her brow.

"Jesus. You're one of those nuts, those radicals, aren't you?"

"I'm a realist, Kate. You moved away from the city too."

"It was my husband's idea," she said, raking her fingers through the hair on top of the boy's head. "He said they would take Jordan away from us, that they wanted to do experiments on the children."

"And he was probably right. They tried to take my girls, too. That's when we left."

Kate was crying now, sniffling and holding her son so close I thought he might burst apart. "He's too young. It's too soon."

"It's better this way, don't you think? He'll be with his father and you, well, you'll probably change soon too. And then your family will be together again. Don't you want that?"

"Stop it!" Kate shouted, her voice strained and her face turning pink. "I'm going to figure something out. I hope for your daughters' sake that you do too." She turned away, leading Jordan back home through the woods.

Mom climbed back on the roof, and the hammering resumed, Becca began pushing the swing again. "She's wrong." Becca said quietly, almost to herself.

"Kate?" I asked.

"No, Mom."

A week later, we heard a gunshot. It bellowed through the woods as birds scattered from the trees like dust in the wind.

"What was that?" Becca asked, pulling the spoon out of the stew she was supposed to be stirring on the stove.

"Stay here," Mom said and ran out of the house, leaving the front door wide open and swinging on its hinges. I got up from the table and ran after her. Becca yelled after me to stop, but I kept going, following Mom's long shadow against the setting sun along the lawn toward the trees.

We took a straight shot through the woods toward the neighbor's house. Branches reached out like fingers scratching at my bare arms as I ran. It was almost too dark to see more than a few feet ahead in the thick of the trees but I could hear Mom's labored breaths and leaves crunching beneath her feet ahead of me.

The trees broke into a clearing where Mom stopped. A little white cottage sat in its center and Kate was standing with her back to us, backlit by a flickering porchlight with moths hovering around it, her hair loose and wild in the breeze, a pistol in her right hand. And beyond her to the left, little Jordan, lying face-down in the grass, a red stain swelling, soaking the back of his shirt. Even from a distance, I could see that his arms were now covered in the same black fur I saw on his neck before.

I had never seen a dead person before. Something about Jordan's body leaking blood all over the lawn made me sick. It looked unnatural, like he had been broken and opened up. I felt bile crawling up my throat, but I swallowed it back down.

Mom looked back when she heard me coming up behind her. "Stay here," she said sternly. I nodded and tucked myself behind a tree, looking out from behind its branches. I couldn't stop staring at the boy, lying so still in the grass.

"Kate," Mom said, walking forward. The woman spun around, looking like a frightened animal with wide, bloodshot eyes and a mix of sweat and tears dripping down her face. "What happened?"

Kate looked down at the gun in her hand and then back up to my Mom. "I had to."

"It's alright." Mom walked carefully closer.

"No, it's not. I was going to leave with him, but it got worse and..." She looked back at her child. "I just couldn't lose him like that. I couldn't lose him like..." For a moment, the wind lowered to a whisper. A branch snapped at the edge of the woods and a giant boar emerged from the trees. He was enormous, much larger than the other wild boars I'd seen in the woods, with coarse wiry fur and beautiful white tusks that curled up over his snout. I thought to myself that he must be their king.

I knew that Kate's husband had changed the spring before. We had all woken up in the middle of the night to her wailing screams and pounding fists on our door. She had followed her husband into the woods that night, near the end of his change, and found that he had become a boar. Dad made her tea and Mom wrapped her in a wool blanket while Becca and I sat at the edge of the stairs, listening to her cry.

The boar sniffed the blood and nudged the boy's shoulder with his snout. When Jordan didn't move, he nudged him again, harder this time, but the boy remained still. The boar threw back his head and bellowed, a guttural, mournful sound that made me shiver, even in the warmth of the summer night. Then he looked straight at Kate, who visibly shook under his gaze.

"I'm sorry," she whispered. But the beast turned away and walked back into the woods the way he had come.

When he was gone, the pistol slipped from Kate's hand and dropped into the grass at her feet. She didn't look back at us or down at her son, just followed the boar into the woods, where the branches and the darkness swallowed her whole.

"When I was little, people used to die in their human bodies. And we would dig holes like this and put them into the ground so they could decompose and return to nature." It was the next morning, and Kate had not come back. Mom was digging a hole in our neighbor's yard, shoveling clumps of grass and dirt over her shoulder.

Becca and I sat cross-legged nearby in the grass, our knees just barely touching. I was plucking blades of grass and splitting them in two with the edge of my thumbnail, trying not to look at Jordan's body.

"Now, if we're lucky, we return to nature in a different way." The sun was high and sweat was dripping off Mom's sun-tanned skin. Cicadas buzzed in the woods all around us.

"What did people used to die of?" Becca asked.

"Sickness and old age, mostly."

"But Jordan didn't die of either of those things," I said.

"No," Mom looked over at the boy who was now wrapped in the blue rocket ship sheets we had found on his bed. "Jordan died a very unnatural death."

"Why don't we just die of old age anymore?" Becca asked.

"We do."

"So, Dad is dead then?" I looked up, shielding my eyes from the sun with my hand.

Mom stopped digging. She thrust the tip of the shovel into the dirt, leaning into it. "Your Dad is a tree, and that tree might live for hundreds of years. So, no, he's not dead. But one day, he will die, just like all of us." She started digging again. "Death is the natural end of all life. We humans used to think we were so separate from nature. We polluted our rivers, our oceans, we let toxic gas into our atmosphere. We made chemical weapons to make each other sick, to kill each other. The change ended most of that."

"Where did it come from?" I asked.

"I'm not sure. There are a lot of theories, though. I suppose the one I like the most is that mother nature is reclaiming us, so that we can no longer cause harm to her or her family."

"Who is she?"

"The earth, the trees, the sun, the stars, the grass in your hand. All life and all that fuels life."

"When will I change?" Becca asked abruptly.

"I'm not sure anyone knows, Becca."

"You told Kate that families change faster."

"Typically, yes. But it's not a certainty."

"What will I be?" I asked.

"Oh, Little Bird. You should be a bird, don't you think? Then you can fly."

I nodded. I liked the sound of that.

"I don't want to change," Becca said with an edge to her voice. She stood up, brushing the dirt from her shorts.

"It's the natural cycle of life, Becca. We are born, and grow, and change, and die. It's not something to be afraid of. That," she pointed at the little heap of body on the lawn, "that is what you should be afraid of."

"Dad said there were experiments in the cities where they were trying to find a cure," Becca said. "He wanted to go, he told me so, but it all happened so fast..." Becca hadn't told me this before.

"We moved away to keep you both safe from all that. It's dangerous there. People are desperate and will do anything to try to stop the change."

"Well, maybe they've figured it out."

"They haven't."

"How do you know? Maybe Kate was right. Maybe you *are* nuts." Becca's fists tightened.

"Kate was very confused and hurting very much, Becca," Mom's voice remained calm, "you have to understand—"

"I think I do," Becca spat and turned away from us, away from the grave, and ran back through the woods toward our house. I got up, unsure if I should follow her.

"Let her go," Mom said. "She just needs some time."

When the hole was finished, it was as deep as Mom's chest. She carried Jordan's body into the grave, delicately placing him into the earth below, like she was tucking

103

him into bed. Then we buried him together: Mom with the shovel and me with fistfuls of dirt. At the edge of my vision I thought I caught the shadow of a boar standing in the shadows of the trees, watching us. But when I turned to get a proper look, nothing was there.

Kate never came back. Their little white cottage sat empty and alone, decaying like a corpse with each passing year. Every time I saw the boar in the woods after that, I wondered if he ever saw his wife again.

Just after our thirteenth birthday, Mom showed the first signs of change. Her eyes darkened with an inky blackness, like her pupils had been punctured, spilling out into the soft blue of her irises and eventually flooding the whites of her eyes.

Becca cried and begged her to bring us back to the city, where she could get help. But Mom said no, that it was her time, and that we shouldn't be sad.

Her change happened quickly. The skin on her arms and face grew dusty yellow fur and she began to shrink in size nearly every day. Two slits appeared on her back just inside each of her shoulder blades. The thin translucent membranes that grew from her back felt like delicate tissue paper pressed between my fingers. The fractured morning light that came through the wings reflected a kaleidoscope of colors on the floor and walls of our bedroom.

Her black eyes grew so large they covered her cheeks. Her nose disappeared and her mouth became a thin line, low on her chin. We couldn't understand her when she tried to speak, but she would hum a low, droning song to us at night as we fell asleep.

I woke early one morning, about week after her change started, and saw her by the window in the bedroom, hovering just off the ground, her naked toes skimming the floorboards and her wings beating so fast they were nearly invisible. Becca was still fast asleep in her bed.

Mom was humming that familiar song, which must have been what woke me up, but the sound was growing louder and less melodic. It was fractured, like more voices with different pitches had joined the chorus. Her body shook and I watched as she burst apart, like an explosion of shattering glass, into pieces that swarmed together into a dark cloud.

Hundreds of bees circled the room together, dancing and swirling around me. They landed on my arms and in my hair. I could feel their tiny insect legs tickling my skin. They didn't sting me, but I wasn't really afraid that they would.

Becca woke screaming and flailing her arms, swatting at the bees. "Stop," I said, grabbing her shoulder and holding her still. "It's just Mom."

We were alone after that, and while we knew how to take care of ourselves, how to tend the garden, collect and sanitize rain water, and forage for edible plants in the woods, Becca wanted to leave, to go to the city before winter settled in to see if they had found a cure. I didn't really want to go; it didn't feel right to leave our family behind and the cities sounded dangerous. But she was my family too and eventually I agreed to go with her.

Becca spent the next several weeks packing bags and making food for us to bring on the road. Every night she leaned over maps of the country, tracing routes with her fingers, a flashlight propped between her head and shoulder.

"Do you remember if the neighbors had a car?" she asked me one night as she made notes on one of the maps.

"I don't think so." We didn't, either. The car that we'd come in years before was rusted out in the front lawn and propped up on cinder blocks, one of the tires now swinging from Dad's branch.

"It's going to take at least five days to get out of these woods. Then we should be able to find the highway and we can hitchhike the rest of the way." She sighed and rolled up the map. "We're leaving tomorrow, okay? It's starting to get cold; we can't wait any longer."

"All right," I said.

The next morning, I knew that something was different. Everything in the bedroom was drenched in an eerie white light. Snow fell softly past the window. It hardly ever snowed this early in the season and I wondered if it was a sign that we shouldn't be leaving. I wandered downstairs, stepping over the backpacks in the hallway that Becca had packed for us, to the base of the elm tree. I sat in between the roots, listening to the gentle hum of the bees, half asleep in their hive in a hollow in the tree where Dad's mouth had once been.

I leaned against the trunk, closing my eyes and hoping that Becca would sleep for a while longer, absorbed in dreams where nothing had changed yet.

I thought about Kate, lost and wandering through the woods around her old house. I imagined that her hair had grown long and turned white, that her pale skin had sagged away from the bones of her face, that her teeth had gone brown, rotted, and fallen out, leaving holes festering in her gums. I imagined her calling out in the darkness for her husband, for her son, but no one would answer. I didn't want to be her, to grow old like that, to rot away on my human feet and be buried in the dirt.

I began to hum Mom's song, like a disjointed lullaby. I would go with Becca as far as I could, but I knew I would return. I hoped Becca would too. And as I laid in Dad's arms, listening to Mom sing, I traced my fingertips along the edge of the gray feather that had grown from my wrist sometime in the night.

See Jess Koch's story "Fur and Feathers"
online at Metaphorosis.
If you liked it, leave a comment. Authors love
that!
Remember to subscribe to our e-mail updates so
you'll know when new stories are posted.

About the story

"Fur and Feathers" began its life as a flash fiction piece about a man slowly transforming into a tree. Both the original short piece and the final short story are from the perspective of his young daughter, known as Little Bird, who soon learns that all humans will eventually face the change into a plant or an animal.

Though I liked the short piece, it felt unfinished. There were new themes and other storylines beginning to emerge from the narrative that felt too confined by its length.

Over the course of many drafts, I found that I wanted the framing of the story to be the relationships between the three women who were left behind: a mother and two daughters. I wanted to explore what happened to them in the aftermath of the father's change.

In the final version, I was able to bring in more of the outside world, to hint at the collapsing society just beyond the woods and to deeply examine conflict within this family following a tragedy.

The story was inspired in part—of course—by Franz Kafka's *The Metamorphosis* and also by contemporary weird fiction in the vein of Jeff VanderMeer's *Annihilation*. It was also inspired by conflicting perspectives on the fear of death and the acceptance of change, explored through the eyes of a child.

A question for the author

Q: Why do you write speculative rather than realistic fiction?

A: Speculative fiction work can, and often does, examine the same questions that realistic fiction poses but it's allowed to find answers in ways that are unbound by the limitations of reality. I find that to be quite creatively freeing. And while I love and appreciate all genres of writing, I've found my home in the strange and liminal world of speculative fiction.

About the author

Jess Koch is a speculative fiction writer and graduate student at the University of Southern Maine's Stonecoast MFA Program. She works professionally as a software engineer in the animal healthcare industry and lives in Portland, Maine.

jesskoch.com, @jesskochwrites

The Lonely King

Gunnar De Winter

Once, he'd had loyal subjects.

Now he only had bricks and sand.

Immortality was not a blessing.

He had dragged his throne to the highest tower of town. It had been an arduous task, but he'd had – quite literally – all the time in the world.

The top of the tower had long since crumbled, exposing king and throne alike to the elements. Mocking desert winds threw hails of sand at the king's weathered face. He clutched a parchment in his lap, a letter from a love long lost, but that too became taunting sand. The king squinted but stubbornly refused to yield to the desert.

Everything blurred to yellow. Fierce, burning yellow. Even the decrepit town buildings had taken on the color of the desert that surrounded them.

Then, a change.

This is it, thought the king. *Madness has finally found me.*

His kingdom, after all, was devoid of humanity. He was all that was left.

And yet, the flicker on the horizon persisted. Multiplied.

The king blinked rapidly, thinking grains of sand stuck to the surface of his eyes.

But the distant dots continued to come closer. They could have been animals, hunting for rare prey. No, the specks were too... intent, too strongly aimed at him.

He maintained his composure even though his heart almost leapt out of his chest. The dots were human – unmistakable now. A few dozen. Even beasts of burden trundled alongside. Druks, judging by the typical swaying gait of the massive brawny hexapods.

Their goal was clear now. They were headed straight for him.

Alone no longer.

Let my reign find breath again.

The king's joints creaked into activity after eons of statuesque silence. He descended two steps at a time. How his mother would have chided him. Such expression of haste was not royal. There was no such thing as imperial impatience, she always said.

But there was no one to witness the childish giddiness of an ancient monarch. Not yet, anyway.

One half of the town's large wooden gate was rusted shut, a giant rooted in the dry earth. The other half barely held on, another giant, one that hovered over an abyss with only a fraying rope to clutch at.

The king stood waiting in the triangular opening that remained. His heavy coat had left a wide trail through the sand that covered every bare surface in the town.

"Welcome," he bellowed when he thought his new subjects were within earshot.

They stopped and looked at each other. Surprised. Uncomfortable. As if they weren't expecting the king to welcome them.

Nonsense, the king thought. *A good ruler acknowledges his subjects. If they do not know this, they were right to flee their faltering sovereign.*

Following a huddle amongst the travelers, the caravan set in motion again.

Then king felt a broad grin appear within the crags of his weathered face.

The leader of the caravan was a tall man – certainly for a mortal. A full head shorter than the king, he came to a halt a few paces away. His eyes couldn't meet those of his new monarch. He rubbed the back of his head, messing up his thick brown locks.

"Uhm... we didn't expect to..."

The king swung his arm. "Leave it be, good man. Say no more. You are all welcome here." He looked down on his new loyal follower and put a hand on the man's shoulder. Muscles tensed under the king's touch. *Nervous, no doubt.*

"Together, we shall rebuild this kingdom."

That night, the thrill of once again ruling more than an empire of solitude spurred the king's rusted memory. He remembered...

The king remembered a time when the desert was dappled with small king- and queendoms, when immortal houses of rulers formed a robust tree of genealogical ties. Each adult immortal had its town of subjects, but kings and queens frequently visited each other. Squabbles were few and the lives of kings and subjects alike were – generally – good. The desert and its creatures were always a looming threat, but the kingdoms were oases of civilization. The king relished the memory. It had been a time of happiness, even of love. Once, he had had a queen.

Then, one day, those lights of culture faded one by one, in the blink of an immortal's eye. Kings and queens increasingly yielded to the desert, leaving their subordinates helpless. Kingdoms crumbled, eagerly swallowed by the encroaching sea of sand. The rulers that remained turned in on themselves, protecting their own above all else. So too did the king. Contact dwindled. Isolation flourished.

There were no more visits.

A true king intervenes as little as possible.

He let them settle in at their own pace, let them find their own place. After all, except for his tower, all buildings were available for use and occupation.

The morning came with new sounds. The grating creaks of rusted hinges, the crunch of sand under boots. The wail of a child.

And was that...? Yes, the smell of freshly baked bread. The king's withered salivary glands refilled, rejoiced. Though monarchs didn't require sustenance, they appreciated complex flavors.

Patience.

For the first weeks, the king simply watched them from his tower. They seemed like ants scurrying under his gaze. When you were outside time, time became malleable. The king's excitement, though, was immortal. Atemporal.

His new flock had established itself and had begun rebuilding the town. Hinges stopped creaking, sand was swept out of buildings and compacted into avenues. A productive lot.

They would need guidance. And he would be their guide. As he was meant to be.

He walked down the stairs for the second time since the new arrivals had entered his realm. Slowly now, regal.

Sand no longer screeched beneath his sandals as he strode across the cleaned streets, a sound he was glad to miss. There was another sound, though, that died as he emerged from his tower. A sound he did miss.

The sound of laughter, of conversation, of life.

The people were still apprehensive.

But I have given them time. Oh, how their previous monarch must have been monstrous. My task is larger than I thought. I shall not waver.

He smiled, ancient creases in his face performing movements they were still unused to.

"Good day!" His voice rang across town. The people cowered.

Enthusiasm can be frightening for those that are not enthused, he reminded himself. *Slowly. Even the timeless can go too fast.*

He took a deep breath. The air was cleaner, full of aromatics. The taste, the smell of everyday activity, of habitation, soothed him.

"I am pleased," he said – softer now. "You have made tremendous progress. This place," he swept a long, emaciated arm, "has not looked this good, this vibrant since... a very long time." *Ward off the sadness, it is not their burden.*

The caravan's leader – unofficial mayor now – frowned with worry as his kinsmen slowly retreated, eyes averted from the king in their midst.

Poor things. How they must have suffered.

"Tell me, good man," the king spoke softly, containing the royal strength in his voice, "what is your name?"

The man swallowed and sighed. "I am Bramm."

"Bramm." The king stepped closer but halted as soon as he saw the muscles in Bramm's arms tense like cables being pulled too hard. "I am no fool. Tell me what worries you."

Bramm's cheeks clenched so hard the king feared his teeth might shatter.

"Fear not, you are safe here. Speak freely."

Another sigh. "We... Our town was ruined by our monarch. He was... not right. So, we fled, looking for a place to be free."

"A wise choice."

"A place without king or queen."

The thought struck the king like a punch to the gut. He stepped back unwillingly. *Heresy!* Rage bubbled. *No. Control. Restraint. Do not lash out. Their trauma is not their own creation.*

"I see." The king closed his eyes and took another deep breath. *Life, joy, the air is full of it. Do not squander it.* "I can assure you that your tribulations are over. Not only will you be safe here, together we will make this place a thriving community where all can flourish."

Why do they not cheer, why do they not revel in their newfound peace?

Bramm mumbled something, the meaning lost in the song of wind and sand.

"What was that, my friend?"

"But we would not be free."

"I... You are mistaken, Bramm. But I understand. You need time to heal from oppression. I can give you time." The king turned a deaf ear to Bramm's mumbling and blind eyes to the man's shaking head. The immortal headed back to his tower. *Free? How can they be free without ruler, without rules?*

The royal mind was in turmoil. Heaving emotions threw up another memory from eons past.

The king recalled one of his mentors, a king among kings, an immortal ruler that had been around when consciousness congealed out of the mists of the universe. As was custom, visiting monarchs often spent time with those in training.

Those with the most thriving, resilient kingdoms preached patience as the main virtue of a good ruler. The king-to-be spent many nights ruminating on his mentors' teachings about the idiosyncratic minds of the ephemerals, the differences that separated rulers from their subjects, and how a true king embraced this gap for the betterment of all.

Days passed in a fever dream as the king's thoughts went back and forth in an endless pursuit of each other. A pursuit without victor. There was conflict inside the king. What he wanted was right there, yet out of reach. *If you can't rule their hearts, your kingdom is empty.*

From his tower, the king saw Bramm hug his wife and ruffle his son's hair. They were laughing, looking longingly at each other. Complete.

There was love, family among his subjects.

Perhaps a queen could remedy the loneliness. Bah, banish the thought. There was only one queen for me, and she is no more.

Now, his subjects were his children, his recalcitrant lovers, his purpose.

Still...

His subconscious violently pulled him out of his reverie.

Something was amiss.

There.

On the horizon something moved. Aggressively, with predatory purpose. Only one thing could move like that. Sandpards, with six strong legs and a muscular body to support a large triangular head that was more jaw than brain.

The king sprang from his chair, ready to warn his people.

Wait. Not yet. Within the blink of an eye, he stopped moving and turned still as a sculpture. *This will teach them they need me. When they see the value of my presence, they will have no other option but to come to me for protection.*

Sandpards always moved in sixes. They were fast. Very fast.

The king chewed his bottom lip. *Come on, misguided mortals, you must see now that you need me.*

Shouts washed towards him like salve being applied to a fresh wound. His elation grew with the panic below.

Any second now, they will run up the stairs, to me.

But no, they ran outwards, towards the feeble cracked ramparts they had not yet completely fixed.

Fools.

A sandpard could scale those easily. A king knew these things. After all, kings and beasts were made from the same sand.

His flock was in danger.

The king roared and jumped from his tower. He called on the power of the sand to guide his descent. Every grain in the town sang to him, danced for him. A small tornado cushioned his feet and lessened the impact on his joints as he landed. He shot forward.

Slow. Too slow. Rest rusts.

Backed by a wave of sand, he reached the edge of town, where two sandpards had already leapt across the barricades. He struck one beast with his scepter. The other one bit his free arm, nearly swallowing half of it. The king looked at the creature and growled.

"I am the sand, I am the desert." The king's arm turned to sand. The sandpard wheezed until its triple double-lobed lungs were saturated. The beast suffocated and collapsed.

The king fell to his knees, unaware of the shocked silence around him. Then came the scream.

The sandpard matriarch had found a victim. The king surged to his feet and pulled his newly forming arm out of the sand. His new limb was still coalescing when he saw Bramm lunge at the sandpard. The man's son lay limp beneath the beast's hungry jaws.

Brave but foolish.

The king knocked Bramm aside as the sandpard leapt. Beast and king locked in a lethal embrace, a deathly dance within a whirlwind. The inertia of eternity became the flash of violence. Sand settled. Royalty and savagery stared at each other, panting. The sandpard mewled. Its smooth skin granulated, cracked. Beast became sand. It crumbled and collapsed.

Sandpards weren't clever, except when it came to hunting. The three remaining sandpards, about to finish the circling movement that would bring them to the other side of town, lost heart. With the matriarch out of the picture, they howled and ran off.

The king straightened and rubbed the sand from his sweaty face.

Now they will understand they need me.

"You demon!" Bramm came towards him, his eyes boring into the king's face for the first time. Anger and grief reddened his face and streaked his cheeks with tears. "We do not want you here. We never wanted you here. My son..." Bramm's voice cracked. "You couldn't even save my son," he continued softly, sinking to his knees. "You can't protect us. You... you are nothing. Go. Just go."

The king's chest heaved. *But I waited for your love, your respect. You want protection without rule? You want the protection of a king without accepting his rule?*

The eternal being bellowed. "You ungrateful bastards! Without me, you would have all perished." The town trembled as the sand shifted. "There can be no kingdom without king. We monarchs are life, we are guardians. Without us the desert would swallow you all." The wind wailed along with him.

The fear in the people's eyes stabbed the king's old heart. Anger and wind subsided in tandem.

As befit a king, he strategically redeployed to his sanctuary.

Suppressed anger and a wounded heart birthed another memory from the sands of time.

The king remembered a queen. A queen many ages his senior, but as striking as any immortal could aspire to be. A well of knowledge that only few possessed. As young king and new ruler of his own small kingdom, he often went to visit her. In his dreams, he already saw their children building a new network of prosperous kingdoms.

The king remembered the first night they had lain together. After the throes of passion had ebbed away, the queen whispered stories to him about the birth of the immortals, myths of how the earth itself – the one true parent of the immortals – had begotten them to keep the desert from spreading over the entirety of the world. The desert, so the queen told her devoted listener, was a cancer, always looking to spread and consume. The immortals were scattered across it to stunt its growth, to provide a counterweight and establish balance. The king and his kin accepted this duty and made it their purpose.

They would not dare!

Bramm's rage had lit a fire in the townspeople. They knew they couldn't best a monarch. But they also knew that without kingdom, kings perished. A monarch would never – could never – leave his town except for a visit to another monarch. His people, though, could travel as they pleased.

Will they really choose the cancerous desert over me? Am I so terrible? Do they truly prefer the uncertainty and struggles of being free from rule over the peace and

*order provided by a king? Bah, good
riddance, I shall withstand the desert
without them.*

The people packed quickly, and the
caravan seemed to tremble with the
anticipation of movement, like an animal
yearning to run. Wooden carts were
stuffed and decked with tarps. Druks were
corralled out of their enclosure and guided
into broad tailored yokes. Before the night
fell and the chill of darkness could grab
hold, the caravan set in motion.

A few people looked back. But not
Bramm.

*He must be a good leader, to achieve
consensus like this, in the face of danger
and uncertainty.*

Everyone was willing to follow Bramm
wherever he might lead them.

*Surely, they will not venture into the
desert night, the time of djinns and
ghouls?*

The wind began to pick up, tugging at
the caravan. The king heard the story in
the sound, the soliloquy of solitude. A
layer of liquid formed on his eyes, not due
to the pricking sand this time, but due to
the sadness of impending loss.

*They would. They actually would.
Perhaps the time of monarchs truly is over.*

Perhaps there are new kings and queens, walking among the people.

Maybe this is my legacy. Maybe they are my legacy.

The king cried unabashedly.

This should not have taken a child's life. I feel the weight of the young one's death.

When the last cart rolled across the town's boundary, a tremor made people's heads turn.

The king's tower shook. From the seams between the stones, small puffs of sand emerged and coalesced into a dense curtain that obscured the tower from sight. A deep rumble.

When the sand dissipated, the tower had gone.

In withdrawal and solitude, another memory reformed.

Then king remembered one of his mentors' final visits and lessons, the last argument before the desert had swallowed the king's only remaining ancient mentor.

Many immortals had already vanished by then, including the king's family and the queen he had loved. Apprehension gripped the king, prompting him to transform his kingdom into a stronghold, impenetrable and towering in seclusion.

His mentor tried to convince him to reconsider. The old one told the king of how, even though they were immortal, they were not meant to be eternal. The greatest ruler, his mentor said, eventually obviates the necessity of his or her own being. Their subjects were the true inheritors of the earth and the salve that could tame the desert. The king had scoffed and scorned his ancient relative.

Their parting had not been not amicable and turned out to be final.

So they have some sense after all.

When the tower had vanished, and the king along with it, the people had returned. Suspicious at first, searching through all the houses and buildings.

They had forgotten that monarchs were creatures of the sand, denizens of the desert. If the king could not watch them from above, he would do so from below.

From his subterranean enclave, the king heard their footsteps, felt them live their lives. Grains of sand were the spies that kept him apprised of all that occurred in his kingdom.

He would build and protect his kingdom. He always would. But carefully now, unnoticed.

The king coerced layers of sand in intricate patterns to shepherd dew into underground canals. Soon, his people would discover a hidden source of irrigation, an oasis seemingly sprung from nothing. When sandpard vibrations woke him from his slumber, he would lay quicksand traps.

My people will thrive. I will protect them.

They will not know. They will not supplicate. So be it. It will suffice for me.

A terrible ruler has iron hands, a good ruler velvet ones. A great ruler needs none.

See Gunnar De Winter's story "The Lonely King" online at Metaphorosis.
If you liked it, leave a comment. Authors love that!
Remember to subscribe to our e-mail updates so you'll know when new stories are posted.

About the story

As most of my stories, this one too began with a single image, a scene, quite often the flimsy remains of a dream. For "The Lonely King", it was an old weathered king sitting on a throne in a half-ruined tower, in the middle of a desert and exposed to the elements.

With that image in my mind, I began exploring how that could be part of a story. I decided to focus implicitly on the fundamental (?) gap between rulers and those that are ruled. Even the most beneficent ruler can feel like a burden or tyrant due to the simple fact of ruling.

Here, then, was the tension that would drive the story. I upped the game, if you will, by making the king an immortal being that had no choice but to rule, a being that had come into existence only to rule. But rather than make him a villain, as might be an easier route, he genuinely wants to best for his subjects. That, however, would mean becoming superfluous. His 'solution' was to become invisible in a way, which is a bit of a hint that freedom is often illusory.

Hope you liked it.

A question for the author

Q: Can beautiful things be funny?

A: In short, yes. A very concrete example would be a painting or possibly a cartoon that is drawn in a beautiful way (what that means is, of course, in the eye of the beholder), but that is still humorous. Banksy comes to mind for me. Often satirical and funny, but also beautifully done.

However, there is also another meaning to 'beautiful', as in awe-inspiring, timeless, breathtaking (say a sunset, Hubble picture, or even the play of light and shadow on a lover's face). In that case- I think- the question is much harder to answer. The reason could be that there is a disconnect between the 'timelessness' of this type of beauty and the context- or perhaps better, moment- dependence of 'fun'.

Anyway, just rambling here. I tend to get lost in thought quite easily. Intrigued to hear what others might think...

About the author

Gunnar De Winter is a biologist/philosopher hybrid who explores ideas through fictional fieldwork.

fictionalfieldwork.wordpress.com, @evolveon

Dedication

For Latska
1999-2019

A tiny Armenian street-fighter, she stood up to crows, rivals, dogs, airguns, and hawks. She never once backed down from anything, and came away with the scars to prove it. Across eleven countries and four continents, she approached life on her own terms for 20 years. We'll always be proud that living (and occasionally snuggling) with us met her standards.

Copyright

Metaphorosis Publishing

Metaphorosis offers beautifully written science fiction and fantasy. Our imprints include:

Metaphorosis Magazine
plant based press
Metaphorosis Books
Driftwyrd
Vestige

Help keep Metaphorosis running at
Patreon.com/metaphorosis

See more about some of our books on the following pages.

Metaphorosis Magazine

Metaphorosis
a magazine of speculative fiction

Metaphorosis is an online speculative fiction magazine dedicated to quality writing. We publish an original story every week, along with author bios, interviews, and notes on story origins. Come and see us online at magazine.Metaphorosis.com

Keep Metaphorosis running! Support us at
Patreon.com/metaphorosis

You can also find us at:
Twitter: @MetaphorosisMag,
@MetaphorosisRev, @Metaphorosis
Facebook:
www.facebook.com/metaphorosis

We publish monthly print and e-book issues, as well as yearly Best of and Complete anthologies.

Metaphorosis: Best of 2018

The best science fiction and fantasy stories from *Metaphorosis* magazine's third year.

Metaphorosis 2018

All the stories from *Metaphorosis* magazine's third year. Fifty-two great SFF stories.

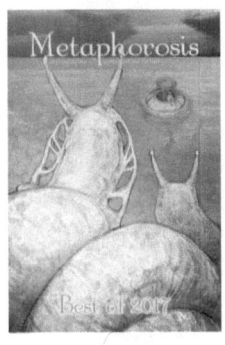 

Metaphorosis: Best of 2017

The best science fiction and fantasy stories from *Metaphorosis* magazine's *second* year.

Metaphorosis 2017

All the stories from *Metaphorosis* magazine's second year. Fifty-three great SFF stories.

Metaphorosis: Best of 2016

The best science fiction and fantasy stories from *Metaphorosis* magazine's first year.

Metaphorosis 2016

Almost all the stories from *Metaphorosis* magazine's first year.

Plant Based Press

Vegan-friendly science fiction and fantasy, including an annual anthology of the year's best SFF stories.

Best Vegan SFF of 2018

The best vegan science fiction and fantasy stories of 2018!

Best Vegan SFF of 2017

The best vegan science fiction and fantasy stories of 2017!

Best Vegan SFF of 2016

The best vegan science fiction and fantasy stories of 2016!

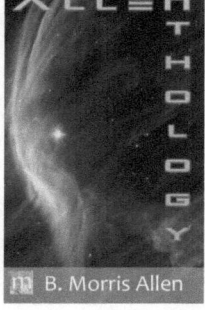

Susurrus

A darkly romantic story of magic, love, and suffering.

Allenthology: Volume I

A quarter century of SFF, including the full contents of three separate collections.

Metaphorosis Books

Science fiction and fantasy books for writers – full of great stories, but with an additional focus on the craft of speculative fiction writing.

Score

an SFF symphony

What if stories were written like music? *Score* is an anthology of varied stories arranged to follow an emotional score from the heights of joy to the depths of despair – but always with a little hope shining through.

Reading 5X5

Five stories, five times

Twenty-five SFF authors, five base stories, five versions of each – see how different writers take on the same material, with stories in contemporary and high fantasy, soft and hard SF, and a mysterious 'other' category.

Reading 5X5

Writers' Edition

All the stories from the regular, readers' edition, plus two extra stories, the story seed, and authors' notes on writing. Over 100 pages of additional material specifically aimed at writers.